AUG 0 8 2016

The LIFE and CRIMES of Bernetta Wallflower

The LIFE and CRIMES of Bernetta Wallflower

* * *

A novel by

Lisa Graff

LAURA GERINGER BOOKS

An Imprint of HarperCollinsPublishers

Library of Congress Cataloging-in-Publication Data
Graff, Lisa (Lisa Colleen), date
    The life and crimes of Bernetta Wallflower : a novel / by Lisa
Graff.—1st ed.
        p.   cm.
    Summary: After her supposed best friend implicates her in a
cheating and blackmail scam, twelve-year-old Bernetta loses her
private school scholarship but, with the help of a new friend, spends
the summer using her knowledge of magic and sleight-of-hand both
to earn the $9,000 in tuition money and to get revenge.
    ISBN 978-0-06-087592-3 (trade)
    ISBN 978-0-06-087593-0 (lib. bdg.)
    [1. Swindlers and swindling—Fiction. 2. Magic tricks—Fiction.
3. Schools—Fiction. 4. Family life—Fiction. 5. Moneymaking
projects—Fiction.] I. Title.
PZ7.G751577Ber 2008   2006103470
[Fic]—dc22   CIP
                                                       AC

Typography by Carla Weise
1 2 3 4 5 6 7 8 9 10

First Edition

To my mother,
who knows a thing or two
about devouring good books

✳ ✳ ✳

Special thanks to Jill Santopolo and Laura Geringer, the two wisest editors a writer could hope to have; to Stephen Barbara, my tireless agent; to everyone at the New School MFA program, in particular Sarah Weeks; to Karen, who sat through the first con-artist movie marathon; to Ryan, my go-to film guru; and to my fellow "Longstockings," Caroline, Coe, Daphne, Jenny, Kathryne, Lisa, and Siobhan, who keep me happy, healthy, and surrounded by words.

Prologue

> **parlor magic** *n*: tricks performed for a small audience

The halls of Mount Olive private school were quiet that afternoon, completely deserted. The students were tucked away inside their classrooms, busy learning the lessons that would lead to successful and fulfilling futures. Calm, peaceful, serene.

That is, until a short brown-haired girl named Ashley Johansson stepped out of Mr. Borable's sixth-grade science class, a hall pass clutched at her side. Mr. Borable had, like any good teacher, given Ashley the pass because he thought she needed to use the bathroom.

He was wrong.

Among the other things Mr. Borable didn't know about Ashley Johansson were the following:

1. When he wasn't present, she liked to refer to him as Unbearable Mr. Borable.
2. She had cheated on several of her life science exams.
3. She was, at that very moment, smuggling several sheets of paper into the hallway underneath her blue school blazer.

After checking to make sure that the coast was completely clear, Ashley removed the papers from her blazer and studied the one on top. Although it had the words "Geometry Homework" scribbled on it, anyone who took a close look at the paper would realize that it was not, in fact, any sort of homework. It was instead a printout of the grades of one of Ashley's fellow students, a tenth grader named Gregory Pewter. Ashley had never met Greg, and she didn't care to.

What interested Ashley were Greg's grades. He had earned all A's in every subject and on every progress report, except English literature. His grade had recently plummeted to a very disappointing B- in that subject.

Technically speaking, Ashley wasn't allowed to break into the school's online grade book during her hour as office helper every other Wednesday, but that hadn't stopped her in the past.

Her second piece of paper, which she looked at next, was a list of school lockers and their owners. She quickly found Greg's locker, number 419, and slipped her remaining papers through the slats of his locker door.

When Greg opened his locker that afternoon, he would find that an extra-credit assignment entitled "Green Eggs and *Hamlet*" had mysteriously appeared on top of his books. There would be no name on the essay, and it would be exactly what he needed to bring his English grade back up to an A.

Unfortunately for Greg, that wasn't the only thing he was going to find. If he *did* use the essay, and his grade rocketed back up to an A, something else would appear in his locker a week later: a note, unsigned. Ashley Johansson had slipped dozens of them into dozens of Mount Olive lockers, and each was the same.

Cheaters never prosper.
I know what you did. Pay up or I'll tell.

On the other side of the note would be a list of simple but effective instructions. The victim was to deposit five dollars, once a week until the end of the school year, in an envelope with his name on it, in a locker in the sixth-grade section of the girls' locker room, number B37.

Ashley had been pulling this blackmail scam all year. So far, in her first year at Mount Olive private school, she'd made what she liked to call a killing.

When Ashley finished her errand, she straightened her blazer and returned to Mr. Borable's room. He smiled at her as she replaced the hall pass on the hook by the door. Then she sat at her desk and began to write a note to the one person she'd kept in touch with at her old school.

> Dear Dimwad,
> Miss me yet? I haven't forgotten our bet. You're going to owe me big.
> Hugs & kisses (you wish),
> Ashley

While Ashley was writing her letter, a girl with a thick orange-blond braid and the unusual name of Bernetta Wallflower was busy taking notes about amphibians. If she had known what was going to happen to her in just a few short months, Bernetta might have paid less attention to the teacher's lecture and a lot more to Ashley's note. But at the time Bernetta Wallflower thought that Ashley was her very best friend in the world.

She was, of course, wrong about that.

1

> **sleight of hand** *n*: an effect performed
> by manipulating the objects in one's hand;
> requires impressive manual dexterity

Bernetta pedaled her bike furiously, her long, frizzy braid whipping out behind her, strands sticking out at every twist. The second Saturday in June, she decided, was far too late in the year to be wearing a trench coat while riding a bicycle. She'd have to keep that in mind for the future.

Bernetta dumped her bike outside the Trunk Number Eight dinner club and hurried into the lobby. She raced past the trick guillotine in the corner, the wax statue that waved as she passed, and the box that appeared to hold a coin until someone stuck a hand inside to grab it, only to come back with a fistful of air. The photos that lined the walls sped by in a blur, but Bernetta had seen them so many times, she could have drawn them from memory. There was Harry Houdini hanging upside down from a skyscraper and wearing a straitjacket, the great Alexander Hermann floating a five of hearts in midair, and Harry Blackstone slicing a lady in half with a buzz saw. Right in the center, just below the sign that read TRUNK NUMBER EIGHT'S VERY OWN, was Bernetta's favorite photo of all. The man with the flop of brown hair and the thick-rimmed glasses, holding a tiny yellow canary, was Bernetta's father, Herbert Wallflower.

At the door to the dining room Bernetta reached into the pocket of her coat and pulled out a glittery pink headband, complete with a neon pink feather, and slipped it over her forehead. She cocked the feather at what she could only hope was a jaunty angle, took a deep breath, and turned the doorknob.

═══════

The room was bursting with diners, but Bernetta quickly spotted her father performing his famous napkin-into-feathers trick at table eighteen against the far left wall. She made a sharp right and hoped her father wouldn't notice her as she crossed to the stage.

She leaped up the stage steps and slid behind the thick red curtain. The clock on the wall read six forty-one. Nineteen minutes until show time. With any luck, her father wouldn't notice her until she was already onstage, holding out an empty birdcage for his very first trick. Once the show had started, a magician couldn't just tell his assistant to go home, could he? Even if she did happen to be grounded.

Bernetta slumped out of her trench coat and adjusted her bright pink sequined dress, tugging it at the hips. Maybe when her grounding was over and she was back on everyone's good side, she'd suggest that her father's assistant wear a less hideous dress.

"Kiddo!"

Bernetta whirled around and found herself face-to-face with Bram Mitchell, Trunk Number Eight's oldest and friendliest waiter. He wrapped her in a giant bear hug.

"Hey there!" Bram greeted her. "I thought your dad said you weren't coming tonight."

Bernetta shrugged. "I decided to make a surprise appearance," she told him.

"How was Elsabelle's graduation this afternoon? Valedictorian of her class, huh? That's big stuff!"

"Yeah," Bernetta said. "Big." Bernetta didn't feel like explaining that she hadn't actually gone to her sister's graduation. That when a person gets suspended on the last day of school—even if she doesn't *deserve* to be suspended—she is barred from attending *any and all school events.*

"Well, I'm glad you made it. Otherwise Todd was going to fill in as assistant, and frankly I don't think he looks half as pretty in the dress. I'll let him know you're here. Also, I've been working on my latest trick, and I wanted you to be the first to see it."

"Oh, yeah? How's it coming?"

Bram snapped his fingers by Bernetta's right ear and produced a small red rubber ball.

"Pretty good," she told him.

"Not really. It was supposed to be a live alligator." Bram's smiling face quickly melted into grandfather seriousness, all concern and wrinkles. "But really, kiddo, is everything okay? You look troubled. Any problems I can help with?"

Problems? Bernetta almost laughed. How about a backstabbing ex-best friend, an unjust school suspension, and an unearned summer-long grounding? She'd like to see how *troubled* Bram would look with problems like those.

"I don't think you can help," she said.

"No?" Bram replied, rolling the ball between his fingers. "I'm pretty good at fixing things."

Bernetta thought about it for a moment. "Actually," she said, "maybe you can help."

"What do you need me to do, kiddo?"

Bernetta pulled back the stage curtain an inch and peered out into the dining room. Her father was still at table eighteen, but the other side of the room was clear. She turned around and looked at Bram.

"I need a basket of bread," she told him. "Table seven."

Bram's thick eyebrows shot up, like two furry gray caterpillars arching their backs. But all he said was, "Pumpernickel or sourdough?"

"Sourdough."

Bram tossed the red rubber ball to Bernetta, and she caught it. "Good luck," he said.

———

Bernetta waited a full minute, running through the steps in her head, but when the clock read six forty-six, she knew it was now or never. Making sure her father was still occupied, she ducked out from behind the curtain and scurried down the stage steps, clutching a deck of cards in her right hand.

She hated to admit it, but she was just the slightest bit nervous. She'd been working the Saturday-night show as her father's assistant for over a year now, but she'd never done any close-up work before. Maybe if she dazzled everyone at the club—showed them all what she was made of—her parents would forget about the whole stupid grounding thing. At least as far as Saturday nights were concerned. She couldn't imagine a whole summer without Trunk Number Eight.

Bernetta was steps away from table seven when she finally took a good look at it. She'd chosen that table because it was as far away from her father as possible, but as soon as she reached it, she wished she'd gone anywhere else. There were eight boys, all around her age, laughing and talking and looking much too cool to care about someone like Bernetta. A slew of blue plastic cups reading "Happy Birthday, Patrick!" had been stacked up to form a teetering tower. At a smaller table nearby, a quartet of adults were clearly doing their best to ignore the boys' ruckus.

Great, Bernetta thought. Her only chance to be dazzling, and there she was, looking like a bottle of sparkling stomach medicine, at a table full of boys. She was just about to turn around and give up when Bram set down a basket of sourdough bread in the center of the table, with a barely perceptible wink in her direction. He left the table, and Bernetta cleared her throat.

"Um, hello?" she said to no one in particular. The boys continued to ignore her.

Directly across the table from her, one boy wearing a green T-shirt, with the words ANYBODY WANT A PEANUT? scrawled across it, reached for a sourdough roll and nudged the kid next to him with his elbow.

"Hey, Patrick," he said. "Watch this." Then he ripped off a piece of his roll, tossed it into the air, and caught it in his mouth. He smiled proudly but then seemed to notice Bernetta for the first time and suddenly began coughing.

"Hello?" Bernetta tried again. "Guys?" She was running out of time.

Beside the boy with the green shirt, Patrick inched his glasses up on his nose with his index finger. "Aw, that was nothing, Gabe," he said. "Watch this. Hey, Dan!" he called across the table. "Do that thing we practiced, 'member?" And he plucked a yellow pepper from his salad and launched it across the table.

Patrick had terrible aim. The pepper was headed directly for Bernetta's face.

"Hey, look out!" Gabe called to her.

But Bernetta didn't need his help. She snatched the pepper right out of the air, squeezed it into her palm, and slammed her fist on the table. When she opened it, the pepper was gone, and in its place was a small red rubber ball. She bounced it on the table twice for effect, then lobbed it over to Gabe. He caught it, his eyes wide.

The table was suddenly silent. She definitely had their attention. It was now or never.

All eyes followed Bernetta as she walked around to the other side of the table and stood directly in front of the boy with the green shirt. Quickly, and with practiced ease, she took the playing cards out of their box and held them in her right hand. It was times like these, when her nerves caused her stomach to turn cartwheels, that she was glad she'd rehearsed her tricks a thousand times over. In one fluid motion she lifted a few of the cards from the top of the deck and placed them on the bottom—the Hindu Shuffle. She mixed the cards several times, and when she was done, she fanned them out in front of him, facedown.

"Pick one," she said.

He opened his mouth as though to say something but then closed it. His unruly brown hair fell in front of his eyes as he studied the backs of the cards. At last he picked one, and Bernetta gathered the rest of the cards into her right hand and began shuffling again. He watched her every move, waiting for something to happen. The rest of the table watched too.

"Look at your card," Bernetta told him as she shuffled.

He looked.

"And show it to your friends. Okay, now put it back in the deck."

When the card had been returned to the stack, Bernetta handed the entire deck to Patrick. "You can shuffle it as many times as you want," she told him.

Now came the tricky part. Bernetta had practiced, of course. But dazzling your little brother while he sat on the couch picking the lint from between his toes suddenly seemed a lot easier than performing in front of a tableful of strangers at a dinner club.

She stood up a little straighter and composed herself. "All right," she told Gabe. "I need you to hold my hand." And then she realized what she'd just said. To a *boy*. Why, oh, why hadn't she picked the table with the senior citizens?

But Gabe didn't even flinch. He stuck his arm

straight out and smiled at her.

Bernetta gulped. Why was he smiling at her? Boys never smiled at her.

"Um, okay, thanks," she said. She grabbed hold of his hand then and squeezed tight, ignoring the snickers around her. "Okay. I need you to concentrate on your card. Think about the card you picked, and I'll be able to figure out which one it is, telepathically." She recited the words as though it were someone else saying them, Bernetta the Great, perhaps, instead of plain old frizzy-haired Bernetta Wallflower. "You have to hold on as tight as you can," she said, "or the telepathic link becomes fuzzy."

Gabe looked directly at her as she spoke, without blinking at all, and Bernetta did her best not to lose focus. His eyes were a very lovely shade of brown, she noticed. Not blah brown like most people's, but deeper. Like chocolate. Hershey bar chocolate, maybe.

Next to her, Patrick lost his grip on the cards. Three spilled out onto the table, and Bernetta lost her concentration for a split second. Patrick tucked the cards back into the deck. "Can I stop shuffling now?" he asked.

Bernetta shook her head no and tried to focus again. She had a trick to perform. And magic was all about presentation. So she squeezed her eyes shut for a moment and took in a deep breath of air. Then she opened her eyes slowly—right one first, then the left—and turned to Patrick.

"You can stop now," she told him. Then she let go of Gabe's hand, although she could still feel its weight in her own. "I have telepathically assessed which card you selected," she announced, taking back the deck.

The whole table watched as she riffled through the deck, and Bernetta could feel the tension as they waited. She hesitated over a few cards before finally pulling out the six of diamonds. She smiled triumphantly. "Was this your card?" she asked Gabe.

He shook his head and frowned. He looked disappointed. "Well, not exactly, but—"

Patrick laughed. "You kidding? It's not even close." He began to make an airplane out of his napkin. "*That* was lame," he said.

"Wait," Bernetta said frantically, her forehead wrinkling as she searched the deck again. "I swear that's never happened before." She pulled out another card. "Here. Here it is. I found it. King of spades."

Patrick rolled his eyes. "Uh, no," he said. "Not it either."

Bernetta showed them yet another card. "This one?" she asked.

Patrick tossed his napkin at her. "Go away!" he shouted. "Your trick stinks!"

"But I—"

Gabe shrugged his shoulders. "It's okay," he said. "Really." He handed her back the rubber ball. "You can try it again if you want."

"Maybe magic's just not your thing," Patrick added with a smirk. "Nice dress, though."

As she slipped the cards back into the box, Bernetta gave a hefty sigh. "I should probably get ready for the big show anyway," she said. She looked back into Gabe's chocolate brown eyes then. "Do you know what time it is?"

"Yeah," Gabe said, lifting his arm to inspect his watch. "It's—hey!"

"What?" Patrick said. "What's wrong?"

"My watch! It's gone!"

"What do you mean, gone?" Bernetta asked. "Are you sure you—" She stopped as she lifted her wrist above the table. "Well, what's *this*? This definitely isn't mine."

"That's my watch!" Gabe cried.

Mouths dropped open as Bernetta displayed the watch that was strapped securely to her wrist.

"How did you—" the boys began. "But how could—"

Bernetta merely shrugged as she handed back the watch. Then she leaned in close to Gabe. "I think," she told him, almost in a whisper, "that you just might find a jack of diamonds hidden inside one of those bread rolls." She pointed to the basket. "That *was* your card, wasn't it?"

And as the boys dove into the breadbasket to find the card, Bernetta spun around on her heel.

A dazzling presentation indeed, she thought.

2

suspension *n*: an illusion in which a person or object appears to float without any visible support

Bernetta's father was standing directly behind her, his arms folded across his chest.

"Um," Bernetta began. She was suddenly feeling just a smidgen less dazzling. "Hey."

Her father tilted his head to a sharp angle. "Didn't I ground you for all eternity?" he asked.

Bernetta thought about that. "No," she said after a moment. "*Mom* grounded me for all eternity. *You* grounded me until my tonsils grew back and decided to pay their own medical bills. And I think I feel them coming in."

The corners of her father's mouth twitched into an almost smile, but he didn't seem to be giving in without a fight. "Is that so?" he said seriously. "Say 'ah.'"

Bernetta opened her mouth as wide as she could, and her father took a good look.

"One of them's come back," he told her, and then he cleared his throat. "But I'm pretty sure the other one will take the whole rest of the summer."

Bernetta closed her mouth and heaved a hefty sigh. "But I'm innocent, Dad. I *swear* I am. I had nothing to do with that cheating ring. I've told you that so many times I've lost count."

Fifty-seven. That was how many times Bernetta had proclaimed her innocence. Fifty-seven times in two days. Bernetta never forgot a number. Maybe fifty-eight would do it. "I didn't do anything wrong, Dad. Don't you believe me?"

Bernetta's father tugged at his bow tie. "Oh, Bernie. I . . ." He trailed off, and his eyes had that frown in them that had been there since yesterday. Bernetta hated seeing those sad eyes when usually they sparkled like fireworks. It made her despise Ashley Johansson even more.

"I can't give up the club," Bernetta said softly. "I love it here."

He smiled at that and tugged lightly on the long

frizz of orange-blond hair that she tied back into a braid every morning, in an attempt to bring some sort of order to the tangles. "All right," he said at last. "You can help me out tonight. Since you're all dressed up and everything. Just for tonight, though, got it? After that we'll need to discuss it with your mother."

Bernetta gave him an all-around hug. "Thank you!"

"Come on, then," he said with a laugh. "We have people to mystify."

As they climbed the steps, lights dimming around them, the audience began to hush in anticipation for the big show, and Bernetta's father leaned in close and whispered in her ear, "That was some trick you pulled off back there, Bernie. I'm impressed."

Even in the dark Bernetta could see that sparkle in his eye.

For the first time in a very miserable two days, things were beginning to look up.

━━━━━

All through the first act of her father's show, Bernetta was so excited, she could hardly stay focused. Not that being a magician's assistant took a whole lot of concentration. Mostly it was timing, being in the right place at the right moment, and standing onstage in a sparkly pink dress. A good distraction is what she really was. But now that her dad knew what she could do, maybe he'd insist she have more responsibility, let her do her own tricks. Maybe he'd even start paying her.

As she handed her father the empty birdcage and he produced a tiny yellow canary to thunderous applause, Bernetta couldn't help thinking about Ashley Johansson. Had it really been Ashley who framed her? Her best friend in the world? Bernetta knew it had to have been Ashley; no one else could have done it. But still, Bernetta was clinging to the hope that Ashley was somehow just as innocent as she was.

It was a very tiny piece of hope.

Maybe, Bernetta thought as she crouched inside the trunk with the breakaway bottom, maybe Ashley wasn't to blame for any of it and was still her true-blue best friend. Bernetta hadn't been able to talk to Ashley since being called into the principal's office halfway through her life science final yesterday afternoon, but she still had hope that once she did talk to Ashley, things would be all cleared up.

An itty-bitty fraction of a particle of hope.

Bernetta remained stock-still, mind churning, as

her father demonstrated to the audience that the trunk truly was empty.

Still, Bernetta thought, it was hard to ignore all those times Ashley hadn't been the best friend in the world. What about when Bernetta had accidentally whacked herself in the face with a tennis racket during PE and Ashley had snickered along with everyone else? And what about the time Ashley told Bernetta she was a moron for not knowing who the Paisley Skunks were? Not to mention the day that—

A roar of laughter from the audience snapped Bernetta back to her senses.

In front of the trunk, her father was pacing with heavy steps. "Well, I do hope I haven't lost my lovely assistant for good!" he said. The audience laughed again. "Let's try that one more time, shall we?"

Bernetta had missed her cue! She bit her bottom lip as her father pointed his wand into the trunk and tapped its edge with three staccato raps.

She leaped out of the trunk, arms spread wide. The stage lights danced off her sequined dress as the audience erupted into applause. Her father grinned too. "I told you all she wasn't lost forever!" he announced. But when he turned around, he shot her a puzzled glance.

Bernetta blinked twice, hoping he'd understand she was sorry.

Keep your mind on the show, she told herself as they headed for her father's last illusion.

═══════

From the audience, Herbert Wallflower's grand finale was always an impressive bit of magic. From backstage, though, it was really more of a team effort, a clock with dozens of cogs and gears that all had to work together at the right time to pull off the showstopping effect.

The lights went up on the stage, revealing a large golden birdcage set against a black curtain backdrop. Herbert Wallflower led his daughter over to the birdcage, where a member of the audience would come to padlock her inside and check that it was tightly sealed. A thick gold chain was lowered from the ceiling and attached to the top of the birdcage, and then the cage, with Bernetta inside it, was hoisted up into the air, while dramatic music swelled all around them.

What the audience didn't know was that the birdcage was nothing more than a dozen flimsy pieces of gold-painted wood. While Bernetta appeared to be standing in a dangling trap, holding on to the bars for dear life, she was really supported by a sturdy plat-form that extended well beyond the black curtain behind her and functioned as a sort of elevator, rising as the birdcage did. When Bernetta's father pointed his wand at the cage and announced that he would turn his lovely assistant into a bird, there was an incredible puff of smoke, and Bernetta would shriek in mock terror and hit a button that released the pieces of the makeshift birdcage onto the stage floor below in a broken heap. At the same time, the platform would shift and whisk Bernetta back behind the black curtain. By the time the smoke had cleared, the plat-form, and Bernetta, had disappeared from view. When the audience looked back at her father, they would see that he was holding in his hand a small, delicate bird-cage with a real live canary inside. Her father would set the bird free, and it would fly above the heads of the diners for a few moments, until it finally settled on the shoulder of one audience member in the back. A closer inspection—and a spotlight—would reveal that this person was none other than Bernetta herself, safely returned from the beyond.

But as Bernetta stood in the cage waiting for some mother of three from the audience to padlock her inside, she couldn't keep her brain from going back to the day before, when she'd been called into the principal's office. They'd been so sure that she'd set up that cheating ring. *So* sure. They hadn't even listened when she'd told them she'd been framed. They wouldn't even let her go back to her life science exam! They'd just dismissed her from the office and sent her home with a preliminary suspension—and the possibility of a permanent expulsion.

They wouldn't really expel her, would they? She hadn't even done anything! And her mom worked at the school as Mount Olive's resident psychologist. That had to count for something, right?

Right?

Bernetta had gone to Mount Olive since she was in kindergarten. All the Wallflower children had. They'd even been given full scholarships to attend—kindergarten through twelfth grade—because of their mother's job. So where would Bernetta go if they *expelled* her? What would she do? How could she possibly—

There was a sudden puff of smoke.

Bernetta gasped in horror as she realized that she hadn't been paying attention at all, and with that gasp she took in a lungful of smoke. Then, instead of shrieking as she was supposed to, she began to cough. Bernetta clutched her chest and hacked, watching as the smoke dissipated from around her, frantically trying to locate the button with her other hand. But she had only the blink of an eye, and before she knew it, that blink was over. The smoke cleared, and the birdcage was still whole. And Bernetta was still inside it, coughing.

She looked out into the audience with wide eyes, her hand on her chest. Then she turned to her father, and he was, as planned, holding a tiny yellow canary. She had never seen him look quite so bewildered.

He turned to the audience. "Well, I—" he said.

But he never had a chance to continue. Because at that moment another cough lunged its way out of Bernetta's chest, and as she reached her hand up to cover her mouth, her elbow hit the button, and the cage clattered to the floor in a dozen pieces. And Bernetta, forgetting in her panic that the platform would be slipping out from underneath her, lost her balance and fell eight feet to the stage, landing on her side with a terrifying clunk.

3

> **false deal** *n*: an effect whereby a
> magician appears to deal the top card in
> a deck, when in fact a card has been
> dealt from somewhere else entirely

"Ashley," Bernetta hissed into the receiver. She pressed a bag of frozen peas against her throbbing ankle and tried to keep her voice low. The last thing she needed was for her parents to hear her from downstairs and know she'd sneaked into Elsa's room to use the phone. The smart part of her brain was telling her to hang up so she wouldn't run the risk of getting into even more trouble. But she'd finally gotten Ashley on the phone, and she couldn't let her go now. "*Ashley Johansson!*"

Bernetta could almost hear Ashley yawn on the other end of the line. "Hey, Bernetta. What's up?" she asked casually.

"What's *up*?" Bernetta repeated. "What's UP? I'll tell you what's—I can't even—how could you—" Bernetta felt like a fish, flopping around in the air, its mouth gaping open and closed. "You framed me," was what she meant to say. "You set me up. You got me suspended, possibly even expelled. You made me so upset that I screwed up my dad's best trick and wound up in the emergency room wearing *sequins*." Bernetta had so many angry words inside her, it was as if they were fighting to see which one could get out first, but somehow all she managed to say was: "You're my *best friend*, Ashley."

"Aw, that's sweet, Bernetta. Thanks."

"No!" Bernetta hollered, then lowered her voice quickly. "That's not what I— You *were* my best friend. At least I thought you were. But then you—you *framed* me."

"What are you talking about?"

"You know what I'm talking about. You knew my locker combination. You asked me that one time, and I didn't even think about it. I just gave it to you. I'm such an idiot."

Here's where Ashley would deny it all. Here's where she'd say, "Seriously, that wasn't me. You *are* my best friend, Bernetta, and you know I'd never do anything like that to you."

Instead, what Ashley said was: "Don't be so hard on yourself. You're not *that* big an idiot."

Bernetta's mouth fell open. It actually fell open, like in the cartoons, when the dog's mouth unfurls like a carpet and drops to the ground.

"You would have done the exact same thing to me," Ashley continued, "if you'd thought of it first. I made a lot of money on that locker scam."

"I would *not* have done that. You're my friend, Ashley. I thought you were my best friend."

"Well then," Ashley said, and her voice was cold, "I guess you really are an idiot." And she hung up the phone, before Bernetta could even have the satisfaction of doing it first.

Bernetta slammed down the phone and pressed the bag of peas hard into her foot to stop the pain. Then she flopped back onto her sister's bed, her long, frizzy braid draped down the side. What was she going to do *now*?

She stuck her arms over her face so all she could see was one square inch of Elsa's ceiling and began to count by prime numbers. One, two, three, five, seven, eleven, thirteen . . .

Bernetta had always had a thing for numbers. For some reason, digits didn't fall out of her head like history facts or grammar rules. Numbers were easy to play with, to memorize. When Bernetta saw the number 14, for instance, she didn't just see a 1 and a 4. She saw 2 times 7, she saw 28 divided by 2, she saw the word "hi" upside down and backward. Bernetta *knew* numbers, their personalities, their habits, and she found them reassuring.

She'd counted only as far as twenty-three when Elsa's door burst open and Colin raced into the room.

"Bernieberniebernieberniebernie*BERNIE!*" he sang, buzzing around with his hands out to his sides like a glider. He came to a tumbling stop on the bed, his face just inches above Bernetta's, and pushed out the last of the air from her cheeks with his stubby hands. "Hi, Bernie!" he squealed at her.

She squinted at him. "Don't call me Bernie," she said, and she snapped her eyes shut.

"Hey, Bernie, why do you have peas on your leg?"

"Because they're cold." Bernetta went back to counting by primes. Twenty-nine, thirty-one, thirty-seven . . .

"Ice cream's cold too. You gonna put ice cream on your leg?"

"Forty-one," Bernetta responded. "Forty-three, forty-seven."

"Or frozen pizzas?"

"Fifty-three, fifty-nine."

Colin poked her in the belly. "Bernie, Bernie, what are you doing?"

"I'm counting by prime numbers. It helps me relax. Sixty-one."

"Oh." Bernetta felt Colin flop down on the bed beside her. "I'm gonna relax too."

"Sixty-seven," Bernetta said.

"Nine," Colin added. "Eighteen. Eleven."

Bernetta squeezed her eyes shut tighter and tried to ignore him. "Seventy-one," she said.

"Six."

"Seventy-three."

"Forty billion."

"*Seventy-nine.*"

"Bubble gum."

"Eighty-three!"

"Walla Walla, Washington."

Bernetta opened her eyes and turned to Colin. His head was tilted to the side, and he seemed to be thinking pretty hard about something. Finally he took a deep breath and spoke. "When I grow up, I'm going to own a hot dog stand."

Then he was out the door as fast as he'd come in. Bernetta could hear him sliding down the stairs on his butt, one thud at a time.

Bernetta resumed her counting, eyes closed: Eighty-nine, ninety-seven, one hundred and one . . . She still wasn't feeling very relaxed.

Bernetta was interrupted again by a gentle tug on her big toe. She opened one eye.

Elsa.

"I heard about your fiasco at the club," Elsa said with a frown. "How's the ankle?"

Bernetta sat up, leaning on her elbows. "Purple and swollen," she answered.

"So I see." Elsa sat down on the edge of the bed, gingerly, so as not to disturb Bernetta's ankle or the bag of peas.

"How was graduation this afternoon?" Bernetta asked.

Elsa shrugged. "Long robes, ugly hats. You didn't miss a whole lot."

"Well, I wish I could have heard your valedictorian speech."

Elsa studied Bernetta's face for a long moment, then leaned back and opened the top drawer of her dresser. "What color do you want?" she asked.

Bernetta thought about it. "Blue."

Elsa rummaged around for a moment, then produced a bottle of bright blue nail polish.

Elsa was always good for a talk and toenail painting when things got tough. Back in April, when Bernetta had gotten in trouble for cheating on her history test, they'd painted their nails a new color almost every night. This time, though, Bernetta knew she was in for the talk of a lifetime. She almost wished she had more toes.

Bernetta watched as her sister shook the bottle, then unscrewed the lid and began on Bernetta's big toe. The paint spread out across the nail in a thin blue V.

"Elsa, you know I didn't do it, right? You believe me, don't you?"

"Of course I believe you, Netta. You're my sister."

Bernetta smiled at that. "Thanks, Elsa. But—I mean—Mom and Dad. They don't believe me, do they? If they believed me, I wouldn't be grounded."

Elsa was quiet for a long time, painting, dipping the brush back in the bottle every once in a while.

When all the toenails on Bernetta's right foot were blue, Elsa finally looked up.

"Look, Netta, it's hard for them."

"It's hard for me too! I was *framed*, for Pete's sake."

"That's not what I mean." Elsa gently moved the bag of peas and started painting the toes on Bernetta's bum foot. "They want to believe you, Netta, they do. But you have to admit there's an awful lot of evidence against you."

"I told you, it was Ashley. I told them that too. Why can't they—"

"It was your PE locker, wasn't it?"

Bernetta rolled her eyes. "But I didn't use that locker all year! I shared with you, you know that."

"*I* know that, Netta, but no one else does. And all those tests and essays that everyone was copying, they were *my* old assignments."

"Ashley stole them! She was over here all the time. She could've easily stolen them from your room when you weren't here."

Elsa paused in her painting, and with her free hand she tucked a silky black curl behind her ear. Unlike Bernetta's mess of orange-yellow cat fur, Elsa's curls were always smooth, each one perfectly coiled like a ribbon on a birthday present. "You could've easily done that too, Netta," she said.

"But I didn't," Bernetta replied.

"But you *could* have. And Ashley's record is completely clean. Sparkling even. You said so yourself. And *you* cheated on that history test back in April."

"It was Ashley's idea. She was the one who stole the answer key."

"And you were the one who used it. It was a stupid thing to do, Netta."

Bernetta knew it was stupid. She'd known it was stupid even back in April. But at the time, when Ashley had suggested it, it had seemed like the only way out. No matter how hard she studied, it seemed Bernetta could never manage to pull her history grade up to an A. And if she didn't wind up with an A in history, how was she ever going to be school valedictorian? How would she ever get her photo up on the wall in the hall of honors, right next to Elsa's, the two Wallflower sisters smiling down on everyone for the rest of time?

"All I'm saying," Elsa continued, working on Bernetta's second toe, "is just give Mom and Dad some time to cool off, and they'll come around. Lie low for a while, okay?"

"What do you mean, lie low?"

Elsa rolled her eyes. "Well, for starters, you might not want to dash out of the house the second day of your grounding while Mom's at the grocery store, bike two miles to Dad's dinner club, and then ruin his big number and wind up in the hospital with a twisted ankle."

Bernetta sighed. "Yeah, okay."

"You're lucky you didn't break any bones, you know." As Elsa finished painting the last toe, Bernetta was sure she caught her chuckling.

"What?" Bernetta asked.

Elsa looked up, all smiles. "It just sounds like quite a stunt you pulled, that's all. I'm sure it was a much better show than my speech this afternoon. I'm sorry I missed it."

Bernetta waited until the cap was safely back on the nail polish bottle before she lobbed the pillow at her sister's head. Elsa laughed and handed Bernetta her melting bag of peas. "Just try not to do anything crazy for a few weeks, okay?"

"Okay," Bernetta answered. And she meant it. She really did.

> **undercut** *v*: to remove secretly one
> or more cards from the bottom of a deck
> while shuffling

Early the next morning Bernetta was sitting on the couch with her toes curled under one of the cushions, a tattered copy of *The Hitchhiker's Guide to the Galaxy* resting against her legs. Normally she was a big fan of sleeping in on Sunday mornings, but her mind had been churning so hard with injustices the past two nights that she'd been finding it hard to get in her full quota of beauty sleep.

Bernetta turned the page in her book and absent-mindedly ripped off a small piece of the bottom margin of the page. Then she stuck the paper in her mouth, and while she read, she chewed. She'd been doing that for as long as she could remember. Her father always told her she shouldn't take the phrase "devouring a good book" quite so literally, but Bernetta just ignored him. Books had a distinct flavor, a certain tang or sweetness to them, and every one was different. Older ones were saltier, newer ones thin like wafers. Her favorite books hardly had any white space left at all.

She was just getting to one of her favorite parts, where the Infinite Improbability Drive turns Ford into a penguin, when Colin appeared out of nowhere and plopped down on the couch, directly on top of Bernetta's bad ankle.

"Hey, Bernie Bernie Bernie, how's your foot?"

She wriggled her leg out from underneath him. "Well, two seconds ago it was feeling much better, thanks."

"No problem," Colin said. "Hey, can I have your shoelaces? You said you'd give me your old shoelaces if I was really nice and stopped putting tape in your hair, and I did, so you gotta."

Bernetta noted the page she was on and closed the book. The wad of paper she was chewing was making its way toward pulp, perfect for lodging comfortably in a back molar. "Um, maybe later," she said. "Why are you up so early anyway?"

"Watching cartoons," he said. He leaned back into the cushions of the couch and placed his hands behind his head. His railroad pajamas rode up, exposing his six-year-old belly pudge.

Bernetta squinted one eye at him. "The TV's not on, Semi-Colin."

Colin didn't seem fazed in the slightest by this news. "Cartoons aren't on yet, duh," he said. "It's too early." He continued to stare at the black screen.

Bernetta just shook her head and went back to her book. She was still reading and chewing, and Colin was still watching the blank screen, when twenty minutes later their mom came downstairs in her nubby blue robe. "What are you two early birds doing up?" she asked.

"Watching cartoons," Colin informed her. "Saturday-morning ones."

Their mother looked at the blank TV, then at Bernetta, as though she might be able to explain things. Bernetta just shrugged.

"But it's Sunday," she said at last.

"Really?" Colin frowned. "Is that true, Bernie?"

She turned a page in her book without looking up. "'Fraid so, Cauliflower," she told him.

"Oh." He yawned and scratched his belly. "'Kay, then, I'm going to sleep. Night!"

Bernetta's mother laughed and shook her head as she watched Colin bolt up the stairs. "Well," she said, turning back to Bernetta, "since you're up anyway, would you like to help me with breakfast?"

Bernetta closed her book and nodded. "Sure," she said.

"Good. I think we have a lot to talk about, don't you?"

Talking? Bernetta gulped as her mother headed off to the kitchen, accidentally swallowing her piece of page 42.

―――

"I have to say," her mother began as Bernetta cracked eggs into a pan, "I was really disappointed in you yesterday. I was disappointed in your actions."

Bernetta heaved a deep sigh. Most mothers yelled when they were angry. Hers lectured about disappointment. Bernetta thought she might have preferred the yelling. She cracked another egg as her mother continued.

"When I came home from the grocery store and I couldn't find you . . . I can't even tell you how worried I was."

"I left a note," Bernetta mumbled.

"It was irresponsible." Her mom's voice was sharp.

Bernetta cracked the last egg from the carton. "I know," she said weakly.

Her mom came right up beside her then and, tucking her hand under Bernetta's chin, took a good long look into her eyes. Bernetta couldn't tell if she liked what she saw or not.

"Sometimes I feel like I don't even know you anymore," her mom said softly.

With moms who yelled, Bernetta realized, you could get mad right back. You could get defensive and shout things out and argue that whatever you'd done hadn't really been so awful. But with moms who got *disappointed*—well, a mom like that just made you feel like crying, made you want to weep big baby tears right into the raw egg gunk you were scrambling up on the stove.

Bernetta blinked hard and wiped at her eyes with her wrist. "I'm sorry about last night," she said.

Her mother nodded. "I know you are," she said. "You're still grounded, though. No more outings for the rest of the summer. And that includes your father's club."

Bernetta sighed. "Okay."

She turned up the heat on the stove as her mother

rustled through the cabinets for flour. "I talked to the principal last night," her mom said from the depths of the cupboard.

Bernetta snapped her head up. Already? Had her fate been decided so soon? "What did he say?"

Her mom turned and looked at Bernetta. "They decided not to expel you from school."

Bernetta jumped at that; she actually jumped, she was so excited. Raw egg flew off her spatula and splattered to the ground. "Really? *Really?* That's so great, Mom!" She sped across the kitchen and gave her mother a hug, eggy spatula and all. "Oh, thank goodness I can go back! I was so worried, I—"

"Bernie." Her mom pulled out of the hug and held Bernetta's head with both her hands. Her gaze was definitely sad now. "Bernie, honey, listen."

Bernetta didn't think she wanted to. She bit her lip. "What is it?"

"Oh, honey . . . they took away your scholarship. For seventh grade. They decided not to expel you, so it won't appear on your record, but if you want to go back next year, we have to pay full tuition. And we just can't afford that. Especially not with Elsabelle starting college in the fall and—sweetie?"

Bernetta plopped herself down in the nearest kitchen chair, staring straight ahead at the wall. "No scholarship?" she said.

"Not anymore."

Bernetta continued to stare at the wall. She wondered if it was possible to stare so long at something that you lost the ability to blink. She also wondered who had chosen the color of their walls—what was it, puce? She sniffled and wiped at her nose. "But that's not fair, Mom," she said. "They should have just expelled me then, if they wanted to. Who cares about my dumb old record anyway? It doesn't matter what my record is if I can't even go to a good school."

Bernetta's mother sat down in the chair next to her daughter and smoothed a hand over Bernetta's frizzy orange hair. "The public school in our neighborhood is pretty good, Bernie. Your father and I were thinking—"

"I don't want to go to that school!" Bernetta cried, swatting away her mother's hand. "I want to go to Mount Olive." That's where she'd always gone. She knew the halls; she knew the teachers; she knew the students. She knew the dress code and which drinking fountain squirted you in the eye if you weren't careful and how to make the secretary laugh so she'd give you a tardy slip even when you didn't deserve one. "I'll never be valedictorian," she said in between sniffles.

"Oh, honey," her mom said, pulling her in close. This time Bernetta let her. "You can be valedictorian of your new school."

Maybe, Bernetta thought. But what was the point anyway? Good-bye, hall of honors. Good-bye, Wallflower sisters' matching photos. Good-bye, everything.

"I didn't do it, Mom," Bernetta said. Or tried to say. Because she was weeping now, sobbing, and really all that made it out of her mouth was a hiccup. "It's not fair." Hiccup.

"It will all be okay, sweetie," her mom told her, rocking her the way she used to rock Colin when he was a baby. "Somehow things always work out in the end."

As Bernetta let herself be rocked, she thought about that. *Somehow things always work out.* That couldn't possibly be true. Because if things always worked out, she wouldn't have worked herself into a fake friendship with a conniving criminal named Ashley Johansson. And she wouldn't be sitting in her kitchen right now, learning that a school board full of stuffy suits had decided she wasn't good enough for their school anymore. No, things didn't always work out.

"Mom?"

"Yes, honey?"

"How much is tuition anyway?"

If you wanted things to work out, you had to do it yourself.

Her mom took in a deep breath. "Nine thousand dollars a year."

Bernetta's heart dropped. There was no way to work out nine thousand dollars. *That* was impossible.

And also, her eggs were burning.

5

> **crimp** *v*: to bend one part of a card to make it easily identifiable within a deck

"Nine thousand dollars," Bernetta told Elsa. "Nine *thousand* dollars."

"That's a lot of money," Elsa said. "What was it Mom wanted? Paprika and what else?"

"French bread. Elsa, you're not even listening to me."

They were sitting in Elsa's car, on the way to the grocery store to pick up some last-minute dinner items for their mother. Technically, Bernetta wasn't supposed to be *out and about* since she was still—and forever—grounded. But Elsa had convinced their parents that running errands wasn't exactly a social activity and that the two of them should try to spend as much time together as possible before Elsa left for volleyball camp that week. After all, it was Elsa's last summer before college.

Elsa turned a hard right into the grocery store parking lot and glided into a spot directly in front of the store. Then she turned off the ignition and gave Bernetta her full attention.

"You know if I had nine thousand dollars, I'd give it to you, right?"

Bernetta realized her bottom lip had been sticking out in a serious two-year-old pout, and she reeled it back in. "I know," she said.

"Look," Elsa told her as they climbed out of the car, "Mount Olive's great and everything, but I hear Harding Middle School is good too. They have a really excellent chess team."

Bernetta scowled at that. "I don't play chess," she said.

Elsa checked her door to make sure it was locked, and Bernetta did the same. "Okay, but— Oh! Remember my friend Gretchen from gymnastics? She went to Harding. She really liked it there."

"Gretchen Weir?"

"Yeah."

"Didn't Gretchen Weir drop out last year to live

with that guy who works at the gas station?"

"Oh, yeah . . ."

Bernetta let out all her air in one huff and stormed into the grocery store. The automatic doors parted, and the air conditioning blasted her right in the face.

As Elsa perused the bread choices in the bakery section, Bernetta pulled her braid off her neck and tried to absorb as much of the cool air as possible. Nine thousand dollars was a lot of money. A *lot* of money. That afternoon Bernetta had counted all the cash she'd been hoarding in her desk drawer for ages—birthday money, leftover bits of allowance, coins she found on the street—and the grand total had added up to $35.22. Nine thousand dollars? It might as well have been nine million.

But still, there must be *some* way to make money. There were twelve more weeks of summer. That was $750 a week. A ton of money, true, but possible. Wasn't it possible?

Elsa finally found an acceptable loaf of French bread, and they made their way over to the spices. Bernetta scanned the labels lazily. Cinnamon, cumin, marjoram—what on earth was marjoram?

She had to go back to Mount Olive, where she belonged. She *had* to.

As she waited with Elsa in the checkout line, Bernetta made a vow. She'd do it. She'd do whatever it took, but she'd go back. She'd find their stupid nine thousand dollars, she'd hand it to them with a smile on her face, and she'd waltz back into their school—*her* school. She'd get her picture in the hall of honors or die trying. It would be a really great picture too. Beautiful even. Bernetta had six years to find a new haircut.

And she'd be so normal, so happy, that Ashley Johansson wouldn't even know what to do with herself. With her gorgeous new haircut and five million new friends—*real* friends—Bernetta would never be an idiot again.

That'd show Ashley Johansson.

———

On the way home Bernetta turned her mind to figuring out how, exactly, she would make nine thousand dollars in one summer. Lawn mowing? She'd have to charge fifty bucks a lawn. Dog walking? That was an awful lot of dogs. Maybe she could paint houses around town. And replace shingles. And wash windows.

Bernetta was busy with her mental math when she noticed Elsa turning left on Dorn Avenue.

"Um, Elsa?" she said. "What are you doing? Our house is that way."

"Yeah, but the music store's this way. I want to pick up this new CD Danielle was telling me about."

"What? No, come on, I need to go home. I'm grounded, remember? And you always take four hundred years in the music store."

Elsa rolled her eyes as she turned another corner. "I do not take four hundred years," she said. "Anyway, if Mom and Dad ask, just say I forced you to go against your will."

Bernetta sighed as they pulled into the parking lot. Really, she was anxious to get home so she could work on Operation Return to Mount Olive. It was too hard to come up with strategies and calculate figures with hip-hop music blaring at you from ten different speakers.

"I'll just be five minutes," Elsa said as she opened her door. "I promise."

"All right. Five minutes."

They headed over to the new-release section, and Elsa riffled through the CDs. Bernetta picked up a CD she'd never heard of from the bargain bin and tried to read the tracks on the back, but her eyes kept darting to the clock on the wall, the one made from an old Elvis record. She tapped her foot on the gray carpet, keeping pace with each second that ticked by.

She was just putting the CD back in the bin when something caught her eye. To her right, not fifty feet from her, someone was loitering in the DVD section.

And that someone looked familiar.

Bernetta squinted her eyes. She knew she'd seen the boy before, but she couldn't quite place him. He didn't go to her school, she was certain of that. And yet she was *sure* she knew him.

Across the store the boy picked up a DVD and studied the back. Bernetta squinted her eyes to get a better look at him. He looked *so* familiar. Shaggy brown hair, deep brown eyes you could almost sink into . . . She inched closer to him to get a better look . . . and rammed right into a rack of gospel CDs, sending an entire shelf crashing to the floor.

As heads shot her way, Bernetta scrambled to pick up the CDs. Her cheeks were burning. She hoped she hadn't broken anything. The last thing she needed right now was to have to buy sixteen cracked Mahalia Jackson albums.

She felt a tap on her shoulder. "You need some help with those?" a voice asked.

Bernetta looked up slowly, praying it wasn't . . . but it was. Of course. Smiling down at her was none other than the brown-haired boy with the Hershey bar eyes. He was wearing a blue T-shirt that read STRANGE THINGS ARE AFOOT AT THE CIRCLE-K. And at last she placed him. It was Gabe, from Trunk Number Eight.

"Um, thanks," she said as he knelt to help her. He placed the *Star Wars* DVD he'd been holding on the floor and began tidying. Bernetta kept her chin tucked close to her chest in the hopes he wouldn't recognize her. As if she hadn't made a big enough idiot out of herself already.

Gabe straightened out a stack of CDs on the bottom shelf. "So," he said, "how's your tailbone?"

Bernetta dropped the CD she'd just picked up. "What?" she asked, scooping the CD up again.

"Your tailbone," Gabe repeated. He blinked at her. "You're—I mean, you're that girl, right? From the magic club last night? You fell from that giant birdcage?" Bernetta was sure she was choking, but Gabe kept talking. "Patrick told me he heard you broke your tailbone. That's why the ambulance came and everything and the guys had to carry you off on the . . ." He paused. "You okay? Your face is sort of turning blue."

Bernetta cleared her throat. "Um, I think I have to go." She pushed herself off the floor and searched frantically for Elsa. She finally spotted her waiting in line at the cash register, and she scurried over.

"Wait!" Gabe called behind her. "Wait, I wanted to ask you something!"

But Bernetta had had enough embarrassment for one day. She reached the checkout line just as Elsa was handing over her CD.

"Hey, Netta," Elsa said. She dug inside her purse and pulled out her wallet. "Something the matter?"

Bernetta shook her head and tried to regain control of her breathing. She looked around for Gabe but didn't see him anywhere. "Nah," she said. "I'm fine."

"Good."

There was a tap on Bernetta's shoulder.

She tried to ignore it, but three seconds later there was another one.

"Netta?" Elsa said as she pulled out her money. "I think that boy behind you is trying to get your attention."

Bernetta bit her bottom lip and turned around.

"Hey," Gabe said. He stuck one hand in his pocket. "I wanted to ask you something."

"My tailbone's *fine*," Bernetta hissed. She glanced sideways at her sister, but Elsa didn't seem to have heard her.

Gabe grimaced. "Yeah, sorry about that. Anyway, what I wanted to ask you—"

Bernetta did *not* want to talk about her accident. She searched for something, anything, else to talk about. "You going to buy that?" she asked, pointing to the DVD in Gabe's hands.

Gabe looked down, as though he'd forgotten what he was holding. "Oh, this? *The Empire Strikes Back*? Yeah. I mean, no. I mean, maybe. I mean—"

She grabbed it right out of his hands. "Haven't you seen it already? It's only the best *Star Wars* movie there is."

Bernetta could have smacked herself. Why did she have to sound so obnoxious? Why couldn't she just have a normal conversation with a boy?

But Gabe smiled. "Maybe only a million times," he said. "But anyway, do you have a second, 'cause really there's something I wanted to—"

Elsa turned around then. "Netta?" she said. "Oh,

sorry to interrupt." She glanced at Gabe. "Are you one of Bernetta's friends from Mount Olive?"

Bernetta shook her head before Gabe could respond. "Um, not exactly."

"Oh," Elsa said, slipping her wallet back into her purse. She studied Gabe for a moment. "Well, Netta, I think we'd better go. It's been fifteen minutes, and Mom might send out the dogs soon. But if you and your friend want to—"

"No." Bernetta cut her off. "No, that's okay. You're right, we should probably get going." She handed Gabe back his DVD. "'Bye," she said.

"But—" Gabe began.

"Sorry, gotta go. May the force be with you." And she turned and followed Elsa out of the store.

It was official. Bernetta *stank* at talking to boys.

They were five feet from the doorway when Bernetta felt a foot on the back of her heel. She turned around and found Gabe grinning at her.

That was weird.

"I really have to go," Bernetta told him.

Gabe just shrugged. "All right," he said. "I guess I'll talk to you later then."

Bernetta shook her head as she and Elsa walked

out of the store. If that kid thought he was going to run into her at any more music stores that summer, he was sorely mistaken. If her mom ever found out she'd broken her grounding again, Bernetta would be on lockdown until she was forty.

"Who was that?" Elsa asked as they made their way to the car.

Bernetta shrugged. "I have no idea."

"Well, I think he likes you."

"No way," Bernetta replied as she climbed into the car. "Anyway, he's obviously crazy."

"Crazy in *lo-ove*."

Bernetta smacked Elsa on the arm and snorted. "He is *not*," she said, but she couldn't help smiling.

As the car pulled out of the parking lot, Bernetta thought she heard the squeal of an alarm coming from the music store. But she was too busy trying to push thoughts of brown-haired boys out of her head to focus instead on nine thousand dollars, and she really didn't think much about it.

> **apparition** *n*: the appearance of something remarkable or unexpected, such as a ghost

Bernetta sat on the floor of her bedroom, legs crossed, and scanned the help-wanted section of the newspaper. A soft breeze drifted in from her open window, flicking the end of her braid as she searched.

COMPUTER PROGRAMMER.

No.

WAITRESS.

No.

CHILD CARE.

Excellent! She could do that. As long as she made at least $13.39 an hour and could work eight hours a day every day for the rest of the summer.

BABYSITTER WANTED. $6/HR.

NEEDED—CHILD CARE. CPR CERT'D. 4 KIDS.
TODDLERS + INFANTS.

NANNY WANTED. $8/HR. HOUSEWORK INCLUDED.

No, no, and no. Bernetta huffed with frustration. This was ridiculous. CPR certification? Housework? And was six dollars an hour even minimum wage?

Even if she found a job that paid enough money to get her back to school, there was still the teensy problem of convincing her parents to let her out long enough for her to go to work. But the first hurdle was finding something she could actually *do*. And that hurdle was proving to be pretty difficult.

She was just wondering if she could possibly, feasibly, *somehow*, pass for sixteen and get a waitressing job when her eye caught sight of the last ad in the child care section.

NEEDED. SUMMER BABYSITTER. 2 KIDS. GOOD PAY.

Now that sounded promising. Bernetta picked up the receiver of the phone that she'd snagged from

Elsa's room and dialed the number at the bottom of the ad.

One ring. Two.

"Hello?" a woman answered.

"Um, hi." Bernetta was trying to sound professional, but she wasn't sure how that was going. "I'm calling about the ad in the paper. The babysitting job?"

"Yes?"

There was a pause, and Bernetta realized it was her turn to speak again. Her hand was sweaty on the receiver. "Um"—*professional people don't say um*—"I was wondering if you could tell me about the job."

"Well"—the woman's voice softened a little—"Hank and Yolanda are five and seven. They're very well behaved. We'd need someone for just a couple hours every Monday and Wednesday, while I'm at my pottery class."

"Oh, okay," Bernetta said. A couple of hours wasn't eight hours a day, which was what she needed, but if the pay was high enough, she figured she could spend the rest of her time walking dogs and fixing shingles. It was a start at least. "Well, that sounds good."

"Great," the lady replied. "I'll need references, of course." References? "From your previous jobs." Did watching your little brother make peanut butter and whipped cream sandwiches count as a job? "And can you tell me how much you usually charge an hour?" the woman asked.

"Uh . . ." "Uh" was better than "um" anyway. Bernetta cleared her throat. "Twenty dollars?"

There was another pause. A long one.

"Well," the woman said at last, "I was thinking more along the lines of seven, but I could maybe go as high as nine."

"Okay," Bernetta said.

"Great," the woman answered. "Can I ask what college you go to? Is it one around here, or are you home for the summer?"

"Um . . ." Bernetta had been trying to sound old, but she didn't know she'd been doing *that* good a job. "I'm not in college yet actually."

"Oh. What high school then?"

"I'm not in high school either."

Bernetta could almost hear the woman raising her eyebrows on the other end of the line. "Well, how old *are* you?"

She could have lied. She could have just said she was sixteen. But Bernetta didn't look sixteen, and once she showed up, the woman was bound to figure it out, and then where would she be? Yes, the truth was definitely the best option.

"Um, I'm twelve."

"*Twelve?*"

Okay, clearly that hadn't worked so well.

"I'm sorry, sweetie," the woman said, and she made the word "sweetie" sound like an insult. "I'm looking for someone a little older to take care of my children."

"That's okay," Bernetta said with a sigh. "I underst—"

But the woman had already hung up the phone.

Bernetta searched the paper for another two hours, reading and rereading every single ad and calling at least half of them. She called about jobs she knew she wouldn't get in a million years. Nanny, housekeeper, refrigerator repairman, youth minister, paralegal . . . she called them all.

Nothing.

It seemed that earning nine thousand dollars in twelve weeks was simply an impossible task for a twelve-year-old.

She flopped back on the floor, legs still crossed, and heaved the sigh of a girl defeated.

Her bedroom door began to creak open, and Bernetta worried for a frantic second that it was one of her parents, and she'd be busted for using the phone. But it was only Elsa.

"Any luck with the job hunt, Netta?" Elsa asked.

Bernetta gave a pathetic sideways headshake and then sat up and handed Elsa her phone. "No," she said. "Nothing. I'm doomed."

"It'll be okay," Elsa told her.

"No!" Bernetta cried. "It won't. It won't be okay, Elsa. How on earth am I *ever* going to make nine thousand dollars in one summer?"

Elsa frowned and looked at her toes. "I don't know, Netta. I'm sorry."

And just like that, she left the room.

She shut the door behind her, and as soon as she did, Bernetta heard a noise coming from her bedroom window, a noise that sounded suspiciously like a person clearing his throat. She spun her head toward the sound, and to her horror she saw a head pop up above the windowsill. A boy's head. A head covered in unruly brown hair.

The boy looked at her, as casual as anything, and smiled.

"I know how you can make nine thousand dollars," he said.

===

Bernetta stood up quickly and backed against the far wall. She didn't care if Gabe's eyes were the exact brown of a Hershey's chocolate bar. This was *weird*. She rushed through her options in her head. If she screamed, her parents would be in her room in a flash, and Gabe would be banished forever. On the other hand, if they found a *boy in her room*—a cute boy—while she was grounded beyond all groundings ever recorded in history . . . well, that could spell trouble. They hadn't believed her about the Ashley thing, so why would they ever believe that some crazy kid had just showed up uninvited?

Bernetta didn't scream.

"What are you doing here?" she asked Gabe. She tried to sound commanding, as if she weren't scared one bit that a boy she hardly knew was leaning into her second-story window, his legs draped over a tree branch. "What do you want?"

"I told you, I want to ask you a question," he replied. He gripped the windowsill with his right hand and began hoisting himself inside the room.

"If you move one inch closer," Bernetta said, "I'm going to scream."

"No, you won't," Gabe told her, slinging a leg over the sill. "If you were going to scream, you would have done it already."

"How do you know?"

He shrugged as he slid the other leg into the room. "I'm good at reading people. I'm like Bill Pullman in *Zero Effect*."

Bernetta squinted her eyes at him. "What do you want?"

He was all the way in her room now, sitting on the edge of the windowsill. Bernetta had her hand on her doorknob, ready to bolt if he came any closer.

"I was thinking about that night at the dinner club," he said. "When you took my watch? You were good. Real good. You must have lightning hands or something."

"That's not a question," Bernetta said.

He scratched his head. "Yeah, well, anyway, I wanted to talk to you after the show, but then you fell and everything, and—"

Bernetta was not going to give him another chance to talk about her tailbone. "Did you follow me here?

Have you been sitting in that tree since I got home?" Bernetta's mind raced, trying to remember everything she'd done in the past few hours. Had she done anything horribly embarrassing, like talk to herself or pick at her sunburn?

Gabe shook his head. "Nah, I just got here a few minutes ago."

"But then how did you know where I—"

Gabe produced a wallet from his back pocket and grinned. He was obviously very proud of himself. "The address is on your sister's driver's license," he said. He tossed the wallet across the room, right at Bernetta's feet.

"You stole my sister's *wallet*?" Bernetta didn't make a move to retrieve it. Her hand was still firmly gripping the doorknob. "What's wrong with you?"

Gabe shook his head. "No, don't worry! I didn't take anything. I didn't . . . I just wanted to see where you lived, that's all." He shrugged. "She probably hasn't even noticed it's missing yet."

"But why did you want my address?"

"'Cause I have a business proposition for you."

"A what?"

"See, I had this idea. . . ." He dug the toe of his

sneaker into Bernetta's carpet as he spoke. "I think we should be partners. Actually, I *know* we should. I saw you at that club, and I just knew it."

"Partners?"

"Yeah, you know, like Bonnie and Clyde? It'd be perfect! Anyway, I wanted to talk to you after the show, but I didn't ever get to, so I thought maybe that was that. But then I saw you today at the music store, and it was, you know, a *sign.* Just like in *Close Encounters of the Third Kind* when Richard Dreyfuss makes that mountain out of mashed potatoes, and then later he figures out he has to go to Wyoming."

"What are you talking about?"

"Look, I need a partner, and you need nine thousand dollars. It's totally a sign."

"A partner?" Bernetta squinted at him. "Bonnie and Clyde? Didn't Bonnie and Clyde rob banks?"

He rolled his eyes. "We're not gonna *rob banks.* Jeez, you think I'm crazy?"

"Yeah. I do."

"Just let me explain what I—"

"I'm not going to steal anything, all right? So you should just go home right now." Chocolate bar eyes or not, this kid was bonkers.

Gabe shook his head. "But we won't be stealing."

"Oh, yeah? What's your great plan then? Worm farming?"

"No," he said. "We'll be confidence men."

"What men?"

"You know, grifters."

"*What?*"

"Con artists," he said. "You know, like in *The Sting*."

"*The Sting?*"

"Yeah. Have you seen it? It's probably one of the top ten best movies of all—"

"What is *wrong* with you?" Bernetta said again. "I know what con artists are, okay? They steal money. And I told you already, I'm not stealing anything."

Gabe's brown eyes lit up with excitement. "But that's just it," he said. "It's not stealing. Not really. It's their job."

"What's their job?"

"They're tricksters. Hustlers, right? But they're not thieves."

"Oh, yeah? Then what's the difference?"

"See, thieves take money. But con artists, they get people to *hand* it to them."

Bernetta narrowed her eyes at him. "I think I'll pass."

"Oh, come on," Gabe said. "We'd be perfect together. I want to get into the confidence business, and you need a ton of cash by the end of the summer. I don't know why you need it, but nine thousand dollars for a con artist is practically nothing. We could make double that in two months."

"Why don't you go con people by yourself then?"

Gabe shook his head. "Nah. A con artist has to have a partner. *Nine Queens*, *Matchstick Men*. Even *Paper Moon*. It just doesn't work by yourself."

"I really will scream, you know."

"Just think about it. I'll give you a day. Meet me at the Championship Mall Tuesday morning when you change your mind."

"Good *night*," Bernetta told him.

"Nine A.M.," he said. "Food court. See you then!" And he slipped like a serpent back into the tree.

7

> ☞ **impossible knot** *n*: an effect in which
> a magician ties a knot in a scarf or rope
> without ever removing either hand from
> the object

Elsa had said to lie low, and she was probably right. Elsa was almost always right. But Monday afternoon after their dad left for rehearsal, their mother had bustled Colin off to a dentist's appointment, and Elsa was away at a friend's house, Bernetta knew what she had to do. And it did not, unfortunately, involve lying low.

She slipped a five-dollar bill from her desk drawer into the front pocket of her shorts and headed downstairs and out the door. Then, with a quick look to the right and left for potentially snoopy neighbors, she whipped one leg over her bike and pedaled off at top speed down the street.

That Gabe kid was an idiot, Bernetta thought as the wind whistled past her ears. She was *not* going to steal. There were other ways to make nine thousand dollars.

She screeched to a halt in front of the ReadyMart and parked her bike outside. Then she strolled through the automatic doors—confident, like she owned the place—and walked right up to the counter.

"One five-dollar quick pick, please," she told the man, slapping the bill on the countertop.

He scrutinized her from under thick tufts of gray hair. He seemed to be trying to figure out exactly how much trouble Bernetta was going to give him. "Get outa my store," he said at last.

Bernetta stood up a little straighter. "Yes, sir," she said. "I'd be happy to. But first I'd like one five-dollar quick pick, please."

He drummed his fingers on the counter. "I don't sell lotto tickets to minors," he said. Each word came slowly and clearly, as if he thought Bernetta wouldn't be able to understand him otherwise. "It's illegal."

Bernetta had anticipated this. But she was determined to get that ticket. Tonight's jackpot was 10.5 million. Ten point five *million* dollars. If she won that, or even a teeny tiny fraction of that, she could go back to Mount Olive. If not, she'd be off to public school. It was up to the lotto gods to decide her fate.

"That's okay," Bernetta told the man. "It's not for me. It's for my dad." She pointed outside, where a fortyish man was filling up his pickup truck.

The old man glanced outside. "Your dad, huh?" Bernetta nodded. "Well, your pops comes in here a lot, but I've never seen *you* before."

Bernetta cleared her throat, her brain churning. "Well, um, actually," she said slowly, "I'm only visiting. Yeah. My parents are divorced, and I live with my mom. In a different town." Bernetta couldn't tell if the man was buying her story or not, but she thought it sounded pretty good. "That's why I've never been in here before. Anyway, he just told me to come in here real quick, and I know he'll be awfully mad if I don't—"

"Why don't you run out there and get him?"

Bernetta stiffened, and the man smirked at her.

She glared back. "Look," she said, her voice noticeably less sweet, "how 'bout I just get a *three*-dollar quick pick? You can keep the change."

The man snorted. "You're some kinda weirdo, you know that? You think I'm gonna lose my job for two bucks?" He shook his head and smiled, showing off his yellow teeth. Then he turned toward the lottery machine, and Bernetta couldn't see what he was doing. "You got some nerve, coming in here like that." He was silent for a moment, but when he turned around again, he was holding an orange-and-white piece of paper with three lines of numbers printed on it. "If this wins the jackpot, you better come back with an adult, you hear me? No way I'm handing out cash to some scrawny kid." He snatched the five-dollar bill from Bernetta's hand and opened the cash register drawer with a clang. "Oh, and carrot top." He closed the drawer without giving her any change. Bernetta grabbed the ticket. "Your pops just drove off without you."

That night after dinner, at precisely eight o'clock, Bernetta sat on the top step of the staircase, where she'd be able to hear the news unnoticed. That was the only way to do things now, since her grounding included the Great TV Banishment. The lotto ticket was gripped tightly between her fingertips. She'd been too afraid to look at it, to learn the numbers that were going to decide her fate.

As the news reporter began announcing the lotto numbers on the TV, Bernetta took in a quick gasp of air. Her fingers tensed around the paper, and she finally allowed herself to look.

"Fourteen," the man on the television called out. "Twelve. Twenty-nine. Six . . ."

When all the numbers had been announced, Bernetta flung herself back on the carpet and crumpled the lotto ticket into a ball. *Loser*. No 10.5 million for her. Not even a single dime. The lotto gods had spoken. Good-bye, Mount Olive, hello, public school.

She could hear footsteps climbing the stairs, and soon her mother was stepping over her. She was holding a basket of laundry.

"Hey, Bernetta," her mom said, "you all right there?"

Bernetta draped her arm over her eyes dramatically. "Peachy," she replied.

"Well, after we put Colin to bed in an hour or so, your father and I thought you and Elsa might like to play a game of Scrabble with us. How does that sound?"

Scrabble? *Scrabble*? Her life was over, and her mom was asking her about *Scrabble*?

"I'll think about it," Bernetta said, and her mom continued down the hall.

There had to be something good about going to Harding Middle School. Maybe they served really good mashed potatoes at lunch or something. And she wouldn't have to wear a uniform anymore. Although Bernetta actually *liked* wearing a uniform. It made morning clothing choices so much easier.

She could hear her father on the couch downstairs demonstrating a magic trick to Colin. She sat up and slid a few steps farther down the staircase to watch.

Her father tugged at each of his sleeves in turn. "Nothing but my arms up there, right?" he said. And then he snapped and produced a banana.

He held it out for Colin to inspect. "An ordinary banana, Col, wouldn't you agree?"

"Yep," Colin said. "As normal as toothpaste."

"Take a good look at it, why don't you? Make sure it hasn't been tampered with."

Bernetta had seen this trick before. It used to be one of her favorites. An ordinary banana that, once peeled, turned out to be somehow—magically—presliced. It had taken her years to figure out how her father did it. And once she'd finally solved the mystery, she almost wished she hadn't. Because all it involved, really, was a straight pin, stuck inside the banana at one-inch intervals and flicked through the fruit horizontally, until the banana was sliced. No magic words, no incantations. Just a straight pin and a little wrist flicking.

Downstairs Colin peeled the banana and squealed as he discovered the perfect one-inch slices inside. *Magic.*

Bernetta leaned back on her hands, the lotto ticket still clutched in her fist.

What was that word Gabe had used? "Trickster"? It was weird, but all of a sudden what Gabe had been saying didn't sound so different from what her dad did every day, trick people. Convincing people that a trunk was completely empty when really his daughter was crouching inside it, just underneath the drop-away bottom. What was honest about that?

What if—Bernetta allowed herself to think those words, just for a second—what if she really did it, really joined that Gabe kid? Was tricking people into handing you their money so very different from convincing people that your father could produce birds from thin air? At least Gabe's way she'd be making a profit.

But no, she knew she couldn't do it. She smoothed out the lotto ticket in her hand and inspected it again. The lotto gods had been very clear. The ticket was a loser, so she was meant to go to Harding.

Wait a minute.

Bernetta held the slip of paper closer to her face.

The ticket wasn't the only loser.

It was as plain as day, right at the top of the paper. The date. It was for last Friday's lottery. The Ready-Mart man had sold Bernetta an old lotto ticket, and she hadn't even noticed. Cheated again.

She took in a deep breath of air, then another one, and another, thinking things over. In the past three days she'd been grounded, kicked out of school, and treated like a leper, and she hadn't even done anything. And Bernetta knew that everyone would continue to treat her like that indefinitely, no matter what she did. She could be a saint her entire life, and they'd still think she was a criminal.

So why not actually *be* a criminal?

The thought was sour, like lemon rind almost, but she chewed on it anyway, and to her surprise it got a little sweeter.

If Bernetta could find a way to go back to Mount Olive and not do anything worse than what everyone thought she'd done already, would that really be so terrible?

Maybe she *would* join that Gabe kid. They'd be

Bonnie and Clyde without the bank robbing. Couldn't hurt to try it, anyway.

Could it?

The more Bernetta thought the idea over, the more she liked it. She'd need a good alibi, though, somewhere she could tell her parents she was going every morning. She sat on the staircase, folding and refolding the lotto ticket into fourths. And before she knew it, she'd come up with the perfect solution.

Maybe Bernetta really was born for this Bonnie and Clyde stuff after all.

She went to her room, dug yesterday's newspaper out of the trash can, and scoured the help-wanted section until she found it.

NEEDED. Summer babysitter. 2 kids. Good pay.

It was just vague enough to work. Bernetta ripped out the ad carefully and crossed the hall to Elsa's room. Her toes curled into the carpet as she walked, every fiber tickling her bare feet. She raised her hand to knock on her sister's door but then stopped and let her hand hang there for a moment.

Did she really want to lie to Elsa? The one person

who truly trusted her? Should she do that? *Could* she? Bernetta lowered her arm.

On the one hand, Bernetta had never lied to Elsa, not ever, not even when she'd had a crush on Doug Himmelbach in third grade—and Doug Himmelbach had picked his nose.

On the other hand, there was no way her parents were going to agree to let Bernetta babysit for an entire summer without Elsa's approval. Elsa was the queen of sweet-talking, and Bernetta needed her help.

Bernetta raised her other hand and knocked.

> ☞ **misdirection** *n:* the act of diverting the spectator's attention away from a secret move

A half hour later Bernetta was setting up the Scrabble board with Elsa and their mother, while her father dished up ice cream.

"Pistachio for you, right, Bernie?" he asked.

"Huh?" Bernetta said. "Oh, yeah. Pistachio. Yeah. Thanks."

Frankly, Bernetta's mind was elsewhere. Mostly it was concentrating on the way her legs were shaking underneath the table and on wondering if her parents were going to notice and realize she was panicked. But a little bit of her mind was focused on Elsa, calmly selecting a letter tile from the bag, not looking in the slightest like a girl who was about to tell a whopper of a lie to her loving parents.

She *was* going to do it, right? She had said she was going to. She'd promised. But what if she chickened out? What if she—

"Bernetta?"

"Hmm?" Bernetta turned to her mother, who was eyeing her curiously.

"Do you want to pick a letter, sweetie? We're drawing to see who goes first."

"Oh, yeah. Sure thing."

Bernetta selected a tile from the table and turned it over to show everyone. She got an L. *L for liar*, she thought.

Elsa drew a G. "Looks like I'm going first," she announced.

As Elsa pondered her first move, Bernetta rearranged her tiles and tried to concentrate on forming words. *It will all be okay*, she told herself. But she didn't really believe it.

Elsa played "waiter" on the first move, and Bernetta marked down her twenty-six points. "Nice job!" their father declared as he took a slurp of his ice cream.

Their mother had just scored seven points for "love" off Elsa's *e* when Elsa spoke up.

"So, Mom, Dad, I wanted to ask you guys something."

"What's that?" their father asked, studying his tiles carefully.

"Well," she said, "I was just talking to Danielle"—*Here it comes*, Bernetta thought, biting her bottom lip—"and she was telling me that one of her mom's friends just moved to the area, and they need a babysitter for the summer."

Bernetta took a spoonful of green ice cream. So far so good. This was the story she and Elsa had worked out just fifteen minutes ago. Elsa had been so excited when Bernetta told her she'd actually found a job that would earn her enough for tuition—"NEEDED. Summer babysitter. 2 kids. Good pay"—that she'd agreed to fib to their parents to help convince them that Bernetta should take it. It was a big fib, the one they'd cooked up, and Bernetta didn't know if it would work. She wasn't even positive she *wanted* it to work. If it did, if her parents said okay, she could babysit for the summer, then she'd be off to the mall the very next day to meet up with Gabe and start being Bonnie. If it didn't work—if her parents didn't buy Elsa's story or flat out said no—Bernetta would be stuck at home all summer, getting mentally prepared for *public school*, her Mount Olive dreams over for good. She wasn't quite sure which was worse.

"Oh?" Bernetta's mom said. "So she wanted you to sit for them then?"

"Well," Elsa replied, "not quite. I mean, I *can't* sit, because I'm leaving for volleyball camp, and I'll be gone half the summer practically. And Danielle can't do it because she's working at the grocery store. They really want someone reliable, though, who's not a total stranger. They don't want to hire just *anyone*, but they're new to the area and everything. So anyway, Danielle was wondering if maybe Bernetta wanted the job."

Bernetta's mother set her spoon back in her bowl with a full scoop of ice cream on it. "Bernetta?" she said. "But Bernetta's grounded for the summer."

"I know," Elsa said, and Bernetta's head snapped back in her direction. She felt like she was watching a play, not a serious conversation that concerned her future. "But they're really strapped for someone, and Netta's got the whole summer free."

Their mother cleared her throat. "Elsabelle, I know you're just trying to help out here, but even if Bernetta weren't grounded, she's only twelve after all, and that's a lot of responsibility, to be in charge of children for an entire summer. How old are these kids?"

"They're about Colin's age, I think," Elsa responded without a beat. "Danielle said they're really great. And anyway, it wouldn't be so terrible. The parents both work at home, so they're just looking for someone to keep the kids out of their hair all day so they can get stuff done. You know, make them sandwiches for lunch, maybe take them to the park or have them run through the sprinklers, that sort of thing. But they'd be there if anything came up."

"I don't know . . ." Bernetta's mom said with a sigh. She stirred her ice cream for a moment. "Herbert, what do you think about all this?"

Bernetta's dad was still puzzling over his tiles. "I think," he began, without looking up, "I think"—he picked up four tiles and placed them on the board—"I think I just earned thirty-eight points for 'kazoo.' Bernetta, write that down. Not too shabby, right? Oh, and yes," he said when he noticed his wife's scowl, "I think Bernetta would make an excellent summer babysitter. Running the sandwiches through the sprinklers. She'll be great."

Under the table, Bernetta's left leg stopped shaking. But the right one was still twitchy.

"So, Mom?" Elsa asked. "What do you think?

They really need someone."

"I just don't know about this, Elsabelle. I haven't had any time to think about it, and Bernetta *is* technically grounded, and—"

Her father broke in then. "We also don't even know if she *wants* the job," he said. "Bernetta, you're awfully quiet over there. What do you think? Also, it's your turn, and thirty-eight is the current score to beat."

"Um," Bernetta said. She glanced at her tiles. She could spell *scam* or *sham* or *scum*. She picked up the *s* and took two points for "is." "I think it sounds good," she said.

"It would be a good way for her to spend the summer, I think," Elsa said as Bernetta wrote down her points. "And it's not like she'd be going out with her friends or anything. She'd be working. Doing something responsible."

Their mother still didn't seem won over. "I know, but—"

"Do you think," Bernetta asked as Elsa spelled out "radios," "do you think maybe if I earned some money babysitting this summer, I could use it to pay for my tuition next year? Then I could go back to Mount Olive."

"That's actually not such a bad idea," Bernetta's

father said. "Earning your own tuition." He tapped his spoon on the edge of his bowl. "Not a bad idea at all."

"True," her mom agreed. "But how much money can you really make babysitting, sweetie?" She laid down the word "measly" for twelve points. "I doubt you can make even close to enough to pay for school."

Elsa swallowed a spoonful of strawberry ice cream. "They'll pay sixteen fifty an hour," she said.

Bernetta's father whistled. "Sixteen fifty, huh? I should quit my job and take up day care."

"Still, though," their mother said, "in one summer, that can't be nearly enough to—"

"What are the hours?" Bernetta asked innocently.

"Nine to six, I think," Elsa told her, as though Bernetta hadn't told her that herself just a few minutes ago. "Nine to six, Monday through Friday. While the parents are working."

"So," Bernetta said, drawing a line in her ice-cream mountain with her spoon, "if I worked nine hours a day, five days a week, for twelve weeks—" She stopped herself, realizing Elsa hadn't told them that part yet. "It's for the whole summer, right?" she asked. Elsa nodded. "At sixteen dollars and fifty cents an hour, I'd make . . ." Bernetta had already done the calculations several times, but she paused anyway, to complete her fake mental math. "That'd be eight thousand, nine hundred, and ten dollars."

Her father cleared his throat. "That's a lot of money, all right."

Bernetta nodded.

"Almost exactly what you need to pay your tuition," he said, picking a pistachio piece out of his ice cream.

"Almost exactly," Bernetta agreed.

"Well," her mother said slowly, "I suppose if you're really that committed to going back to Mount Olive, and if you can show us that you can truly be responsible and work very hard all summer . . ." She took a long, deep breath, and Bernetta's leg shook harder than ever. "I guess in that case it's all right with me if you want to take the job. If you can really make that kind of money babysitting, I think it would be an excellent idea to put it toward your education."

Bernetta clapped her hands. "Oh, Mom! Thank you *so* much! It's okay with you too, right, Dad?"

But her father didn't seem to be paying any attention. He was leaning across the table, studying Bernetta's scoring.

"Dad?" Bernetta tried again.

Elsa set down her ice-cream spoon. "Something wrong, Dad?" she asked.

He pushed his glasses up on his nose with his index finger. "I'm just wondering where my points went, that's all."

"What do you mean?" Bernetta asked. "Your points are right here. Thirty-eight—I wrote it down."

"No, not those," he said. "My other points. For my second move."

"Um, Dad?" Elsa said. "You've only gone once."

"No," he said, looking genuinely puzzled. "No, I could have sworn I went again. I even got the fifty-point bonus for using all my letters. I'd bet my life on it."

Bernetta's mother shook her head, but she was smiling just the same. "There are no new words on the board, dear. I think you're losing your senses a little early."

"Or trying to cheat," Elsa said with a snort.

"Well, if I didn't play a word," their father replied, "then where did all my letters go?" He pointed to his tray, where not one tile remained. "See?" he told them. "Not crazy. My letters must have vanished."

Elsa laughed. "Right," she said. "They just flew off the table."

"Nah," he said, rubbing his chin. "I bet Bernetta stole them. To make up for her lousy two points. I bet she's hiding them. Lift up your ice-cream bowl, please, missy. I bet you've stowed them under there."

"*Dad*," Bernetta said with a laugh, "I did not—"

"Up, please!"

Bernetta lifted her ice-cream bowl. No letters.

"Hmm," her father said. "Well, that's funny, I could have sworn . . ." He searched the table, looking under the box top, under his wife's elbow, inside Elsa's dictionary.

"What's the missing word, dear?" her mother asked. "Maybe that would help."

"It was . . ." He reached across the table and swooped up Bernetta's crumpled napkin. "Well, there it is, right there."

And sure enough, underneath the napkin, spelled out crookedly across the table, lay the word "cunning."

"I'd like my eighty-nine points, please," Bernetta's father said with the slightest of smiles. And as he set his tiles carefully on the board, turning "love" into "clove," he added, "And, Bernie, of course you can take that job. I think it's a wonderful idea."

She grinned and wrote down his score, secretly adding an extra five points for a trick well done.

The next morning Bernetta gulped down her cereal
as quickly as possible. She wanted to be out the
door and on her way to the mall before her parents came
back into the kitchen and decided to ask her more questions about babysitting. After she'd inhaled the last
spoonful, she lurched her chair back across the tiled floor
with a screech and dumped her bowl in the sink. "'Bye,
everyone!" she called into the living room, slinging her
backpack over her shoulder. "I'm off to babysit!"

Her mother hurried into the kitchen before
Bernetta made it out the door. "Are you positive you
don't want a ride over there?" she asked for the fif-
teenth time.

"It's fine, Mom," Bernetta told her. "I'll just take

my bike. It's not that far. Besides, I don't want to make Colin late for his swim lesson."

"All right, then," her mom replied. She gave Bernetta a kiss on the forehead. "Have a good time with the kids. And call me if you need anything. Or if the parents get sick, or if you'll be home late."

"Or if there's a fire. Okay, Mom."

"'Bye, sweetie. I love you!"

She gave her mother a quick hug. "Love you too," she said, and hustled out the door.

———

Bernetta worked up quite a sweat pedaling her way to the mall, but she arrived at the food court at precisely nine o'clock. Gabe was waiting by the pretzel stand, his hands in the pockets of his jeans. Today his T-shirt was red, and scrolled across it were the words YOUR CAR'S UGLIER THAN I AM. He saw her coming and waved her over.

"Hey!" he greeted her, his eyes sparkling. "You came!"

"Yeah."

"You ready for your first lesson?"

"Um, lesson?"

"Yeah. I thought I could teach you some moves,

and then we'll get started right away. Don't worry, you'll be a natural. Oh, and before we start, I think we should agree to a fifty-fifty split of all profits. Deal?"

Bernetta raised an eyebrow as Gabe led her over to a table with two chairs. "Are you some kind of professional thief or something?" They sat.

"Nah." Gabe grinned. "I guess I've just done a lot of research."

"What do you mean, research?" Bernetta cocked her head to the side and studied him. "You mean watching movies, don't you? Con artist ones, like what you were talking about the other day. Is that how you *researched* everything, watching movies?"

Gabe shrugged. "Yeah, so?"

"You some kind of film buff or something?"

He placed his hands flat on the table. "Name a movie, one you think I've never seen. I'll bet you five bucks I can say at least one line from it."

Bernetta wrinkled her nose. Granted, back at Mount Olive, she hadn't talked to a whole lot of boys, but she'd never had any idea they were this weird. "Um . . ." She named the first movie that popped into her head. "*Apollo 13*?" Her parents had rented that one last week.

"You're kidding, right?" Gabe asked, eyebrows raised high.

"Look, if you don't know it, it's fine, we can just—"

"'Houston, we have a problem.' That'll be five bucks, please."

Gabe held out his hand, but Bernetta just rolled her eyes at him. "I don't have five bucks," she said. "That's why I'm here."

"All right, you can owe me," Gabe said. He shook his head and laughed. "Man, I can't believe you picked *Apollo 13*! Anyway, you ready to learn the shortchange?"

"Shortchange?"

"Yeah. It's probably the most basic con there is. But you still have to be a pretty good talker to make it work. Otherwise people start to get suspicious. Here." He took his wallet out of the front pocket of his jeans and began riffling through the bills inside. There were a lot of bills. He pulled out a couple. "Say you're the cashier and I'm the customer, and—"

"Wait," Bernetta said. This was all going so fast. "Just hold on a second."

"What?" Gabe asked. "What is it?"

"It's just . . ." Bernetta traced her finger over a crack in the table. "I mean, okay, I get it, you've seen a lot of movies. But have you ever actually"—she lowered her voice—"*stolen* anything before? Because it's probably a lot different from in the movies."

Gabe leaned forward. "I already told you," he said. "We're not gonna be stealing. It's *conning*. And anyway, yes, I have stolen stuff before."

"Really?"

"Yeah."

Bernetta gulped.

Gabe set the bills from his wallet carefully on the table. "Okay, so with the shortchange," he said, "what happens is you pay for something with a ten-dollar bill and get a twenty back as change."

Bernetta tried to wrap her head around that. "Wait. You mean, I can buy something and get more money back than I paid in the first place?"

"Sure. You have to know how to read people, though. The best way is to try it on someone who's new at their job or really busy or something."

Bernetta nodded slowly. It was a lot like working at the magic club. You wanted to catch people off guard. Make them check up your sleeves for the ace when really you had three hidden in your coat pocket. "Got it," she said. And then she paused. "Wait."

Gabe frowned. "Yeah?"

"What's your deal anyway?"

"My deal?" Gabe asked.

"Yeah. I mean, I'm here because I lost my scholarship, but what about you? Why do *you* want to be a con artist so bad?"

"Okay," Gabe said. "I guess that's a good question." He shuffled the bills around on the table as he spoke. "See, my family's rich. Completely loaded. I'm like Veruca Salt in *Willy Wonka and the Chocolate Factory*. But well, when I was little, I hardly ever got to see my parents. I just had to hang out with the nanny all the time. So *now*"—he looked up at her—"now I steal stuff because no one ever loved me."

Bernetta took a good look into his chocolate brown eyes. "Is that true?" she asked.

He grinned. "Maybe."

"All right, fine," Bernetta said with a laugh. "Show me this shortchange thing. I'm the cashier and you're—"

"Wait," Gabe said. "I have to ask *you* a question now."

Bernetta was pretty sure a smile was creeping its way onto her face. There was nothing she could do about it, really. "You do?"

"Yes, I do. Two of them actually."

"Well," Bernetta said, folding her arms in front of her in mock annoyance, "what are they then?"

"One. What's your name?"

"My name?"

"Yeah, you never told me."

"Bernetta."

"Ber what?"

"Bernetta. That's my name."

Gabe stared at her for a moment, and Bernetta couldn't tell what he was thinking. *"Bernetta?"* he repeated.

"Yeah."

"Wow," Gabe said.

"What?"

"Nothing," he replied, but then he laughed, a quick chortle that started in his throat and came out his nose.

"What?"

Gabe shook his head. "It's just the most terrible name I've ever heard, that's all. *Bernetta?* Man, that's rough."

Bernetta probably should have been offended by that. But she wasn't. She'd hated her name her whole life. Most people tried to tell Bernetta her name was "unusual" or "dignified," but that didn't fool her. At least Gabe was honest.

"My great-uncle Bernard died three weeks before I was born," she explained.

"Good thing his name wasn't Mortimer," Gabe replied.

Bernetta thought about that. "Or Wally. *That* would've been awful."

"I don't know," Gabe said. "I think you'd make a really nice Wallamina."

Bernetta laughed again. "All right, all right," she said. "What was your second question?"

"Want to bet me double or nothing I can't guess another movie quote?"

Bernetta thought about it. "That's your question?" He nodded. "All right, fine." She tried to come up with one he probably hadn't seen. "*The Muppets Take Manhattan,*" she said at last. She and Elsa used to watch that movie all the time when they were little. It had been their favorite for years. It was probably too goofy for some sophisticated film addict like Gabe.

"'Ocean Breeze soap,'" he said. "'It's just like taking an ocean cruise, only there's no boat and you don't actually go anywhere.' Too easy. That's ten bucks you owe me now, Wallamina."

Bernetta stuck her elbows on the table and pressed

her hands under her chin. "All right," she said. "Teach me this shortchange thing before I owe you my entire tuition."

———

After running through the moves of the shortchange with Gabe for about twenty minutes, Bernetta was pretty sure she had it down. Together they left the food court and scoped out a location for Bernetta to pull her first con.

They finally decided to try the candy store. The teenage girl behind the counter was on the phone, and she didn't seem to be paying much attention to anything but her conversation.

"Wish me luck," Bernetta whispered as Gabe nudged her into the store.

"You'll be fine," Gabe replied, "Don't even worry. Just do like I told you."

Bernetta entered the store on wobbly legs, but she did her best to hide it.

"Look, Tiffany," the girl behind the counter was saying into the phone, "it's not like that, all right? Me and Jeremy are just friends."

Bernetta selected a pack of gum from the rack under the counter and placed it in front of the girl. Her name tag said HEATHER.

"Tiff, hold on a sec. I got to ring someone up."

Heather gripped the phone between her chin and her shoulder. "You want a bag for that?" she asked Bernetta.

"No, thanks."

"Eighty-nine cents." She rang up the order, and the drawer clanged open. "Tiff, that's not what I'm saying. Cheryl told Beth that Jeremy said that *you* . . . hold on."

Bernetta handed Heather a ten-dollar bill, and she took it, then snapped the bills out of the drawer to make change. A five, four ones, and eleven cents.

"Here you go," she told Bernetta, handing her the change.

But Bernetta had already pulled another one-dollar bill out of her pocket. "Sorry, I—"

Her ear still wedged into the phone, Heather's head shot up to look at Bernetta.

"Sorry," Bernetta repeated. She added her dollar to the bills already on the counter and plopped her hand on top of the pile. "Can I trade these bills for a ten?"

Heather glanced at the pile and nodded. "Tiffany, *no*. That's not what I said at all. Well, then Beth's a liar." She handed Bernetta a ten-dollar bill.

"Thanks." Bernetta took the ten and moved to put it in her pocket but then paused, as though something had just occurred to her. *Here's where the trick comes in*, Bernetta thought. She had to keep calm and act normal. It was just like fanning out a deck of cards before an audience member when the whole time the guy had no idea the deck contained nothing but aces.

Bernetta wondered if Gabe could see her from outside the store. She wondered if his heart was dancing the cha-cha like hers was.

"Actually," she told Heather, scooping up the pile of bills still on the counter and placing her ten on top, "this is a lot of change. Can I just get a twenty?"

Heather hardly looked at Bernetta as she took the bills. "She did not say that. She did not! Tiffany, you *know* that's not true." She handed Bernetta a twenty-dollar bill and closed the drawer.

Bernetta walked out of the store with a pack of gum in her left pocket and a twenty-dollar bill in her right, $9.11 richer than when she'd entered. Her heart was gradually slowing its way into more of a Viennese waltz.

"See?" Gabe said when she reached him. He was grinning. "You were great! You're practically Mel Gibson in *Maverick*. I knew you'd be a natural."

Bernetta couldn't help returning the smile. At this rate, there was nothing in the world that could stop her from heading back to Mount Olive.

10

A s the morning wore on, and the wad of twenty-
dollar bills grew ever larger in her backpack,
Bernetta began to feel more and more confident. Gabe
was a good teacher. Shortly after one o'clock they
were standing outside the arcade, where Gabe had
promised to show her a new trick.

"Hey, Gabe?" Bernetta was standing right next to
him, but the beeps and buzzes from the arcade made
it hard to have a quiet conversation. "What are we
looking for, anyway?"

"Bad eyesight," he told her. "You're gonna love
this next trick. It's really cool."

Gabe was focused on the crowd passing by, and

Bernetta took the opportunity to study him. The flashing lights from the games inside bounced across his face, changing the skin on his cheek from green to red to blue.

"So," Bernetta hollered across to him, "where do you get all those T-shirts you have anyway? Are they all movie quotes?"

Gabe kept his eyes steady on the crowd, but he nodded in Bernetta's direction. "Yeah. Aren't they great? My friend Patrick's dad owns a silk-screening shop. I make them all myself. You want one?"

Bernetta shook her head. "Nah, I think I'm okay."

Gabe didn't say anything to that, so Bernetta tried to think of something else to fill the conversation gap. Maybe when she got home, she'd have Elsa give her a lesson in How to Talk to Boys. "So, um . . ." Bernetta said. "That one you're wearing, 'Your car's uglier than I am.' What movie's that from?"

Gabe glanced down, as though he'd forgotten what shirt he'd put on that morning. "Really? You don't know? It's *American Graffiti*."

"Oh," Bernetta said. "I've never seen it."

He turned to look at her at last, his hands in his pockets. "Are you *serious*? You've really never seen it?"

Bernetta shook her head and silently cursed herself. *Why* hadn't she ever seen that movie? If she had, then she and Gabe would be able to talk for hours probably.

"Well, I'll have to lend it to you then. I have it at my house."

"Oh, okay," Bernetta said. "Cool."

Gabe went back to watching the crowd. "You've seen *The Godfather*, though, right?" he said.

"Um, isn't that rated R or something?" Bernetta asked. "I'm not allowed to watch R-rated movies."

"Wait, really?" Gabe said. He seemed truly shocked. "Then what do you *do*?"

Bernetta rolled her eyes. "Not everyone's obsessed with movies, you know," she said with a laugh. "There's other stuff to do too. Like reading a book or something."

"No way," Gabe said, but he was grinning. "No way can a book be better than a movie."

"It's possible," Bernetta said. It was funny, she thought, how arguing with Gabe could actually be fun. Normally she hated arguing.

"Name one," Gabe challenged.

"*A Wrinkle in Time.*"

"I've never read it."

"Well, you should. It's amazing."

He smiled at her for a second. But just as the butterflies let loose in Bernetta's middle, Gabe caught sight of something over her shoulder, and the moment was over.

"I found them," Gabe said. "Perfect. That old guy looks exactly like the uncle from *American Movie*."

"What?"

Instead of answering, Gabe ducked inside the arcade, grabbing Bernetta by the elbow so that she followed with an awkward tumble. As soon as they were inside, he led her right back out the door. An elderly couple was approaching, not ten feet away. Gabe put on a friendly smile and headed over to them. Bernetta was right on his heels.

"Oh," Gabe declared suddenly, as though something had just occurred to him. He stopped dead in his tracks and looked at Bernetta. "Maybe we should ask them, Patty." He pointed to the old couple.

Patty?

"Excuse me?" Gabe said to the couple just as they passed by.

The couple stopped, and the old woman smiled at

them, peering out from behind tiny rectangular glasses. "Yes, dear?" she said to Gabe.

Gabe shuffled his feet, doing what Bernetta thought was a very good impersonation of someone who didn't want to be any bother. He was a pretty good actor, actually. Maybe, if someone decided to make a new movie of *A Wrinkle in Time*, he could play Calvin. Although Calvin was tall and skinny with bright blue eyes and red hair, so maybe that wouldn't entirely . . .

Bernetta shook her head and tried to focus on the scene in front of her.

"I'm sorry to bug you like this," Gabe said, "but . . ." He shook his head. "Oh, never mind, it's stupid. Sorry." He began to walk on again, but the old man stopped him.

"No bother, young man!" he said. His voice was thick and bellowy, like a tractor driving over gravel. "What's the trouble?"

"Well, it's just . . ." Gabe scratched his arm. "See, we're here with Patty's little sister . . ." He pointed to Bernetta. "It's her birthday tomorrow, and she really likes to play pinball and—"

"Isn't that sweet!" the old woman said.

"Anyway," Gabe went on, "all we have is this

twenty that Patty's mom gave us"—he produced the bill from his pocket—"for the games. But the change machine's busted, and the guy behind the counter says he's low on quarters, so he'll only give us change for a ten. Could you . . . oh, never mind, it's too much trouble. I'll just try over at the bookstore."

What was he up to? Bernetta wondered. Was he going to catch the man off guard and steal his wallet? Is that how they did things in *The Godfather*?

"Now, now," the old man shouted. "Just you hang on there. I can give you change, no need to wait in that line. Let's see now." He reached his hand into the pocket of his perfectly creased maroon slacks and pulled out a wad of bills. "Here you go, young man," he said. He counted out one ten and two fives. "They ought to change that for you, right?"

"I think so."

"Give the kids some quarters too, Paul," the old woman instructed, peering over her husband's shoulder. She looked at Bernetta and winked. "He's always carrying around so much change. Good to get rid of it. Then maybe he won't jangle so much."

Bernetta smiled back weakly. She didn't know what Gabe was planning, but she had a sinking feeling that when it was over, this old couple wouldn't think they were quite so cute anymore.

"Yes, yes," her husband said. He dug into his other pocket and pulled out a handful of change, then plucked out all the quarters he could find. Bernetta counted as he did. Seven. "Will dimes help you any?" he asked them.

The woman shook her head. "Oh, Paul, you know all those games only take quarters now."

"Yes, indeed, these days!" the man hollered. "But you know"—he leaned in close to Bernetta and Gabe, as though to tell them a secret—"it wasn't that long ago skee ball cost a nickel. You remember that, Margaret? You remember when skee ball only cost a nickel?"

"I do, I do."

"Here you go," he told them, handing over the money. "The extra change is on me."

Gabe took the money and handed him the twenty. Bernetta kept a careful eye on him the whole time, but he didn't slip any hundreds out of the man's pocket or rip off the woman's gold bracelet. All he did was hand over the twenty-dollar bill and take the change. Maybe his conscience had suddenly kicked in or something.

Thank goodness, Bernetta thought. She needed

money for Mount Olive, but she wasn't ready to rip off a sweet elderly couple to get there.

"Thank you very much," Gabe said, pocketing the money.

"Not a problem," the man answered. "And you just wait. One day skee ball will cost five dollars a game, and you'll be out here in the mall telling some youngsters that you remember when it only cost a *quarter*! Ha!" And they walked away.

Bernetta turned to Gabe as he tucked the money in his pocket. "Well, they seemed nice," she said. "I guess you decided not to pull anything on them after all, huh?"

"Are you kidding me?" Gabe replied. "That old grandpa just traded me twenty-one dollars and seventy-five cents for a two-dollar bill. I mean, I glued the corners of four different twenties to it, but you'd still have to be totally blind not to notice. Biggest profit we've made all day."

"But . . ." Bernetta sputtered. "I can't believe you just—I mean, they were so *nice*."

Gabe nodded. "Yeah, but completely rich. Did you see that lady's bracelet?"

"But . . ." Bernetta began again.

Gabe just smiled at her. "So this book?" he said, his head tilted to the side. "*A Wrinkle in Time*? You think I should read it?"

"Um . . ." Bernetta bit at the skin around her right thumbnail. She knew there was something she wanted to say to Gabe, something to tell him exactly how she felt about swindling old people. But for some reason the words seemed to be slowly melting together in her brain, and she was having trouble piecing them together to make a sentence.

Maybe his eyes were darker than a Hershey bar, she thought. Maybe they were more of a rich Ghirardelli's.

"Um, yeah," she replied at last. "It's a really good book. You'd like it."

"Cool," Gabe said. "Let's go see if they have it in the bookstore. Oh, and there's another trick I want to show you. I think you'll be really good at it."

Definitely Ghirardelli's, Bernetta decided as she followed Gabe through the mall.

11

As soon as they set foot inside the bookstore, they headed over to the fantasy and science fiction section. Bernetta scanned the authors until she found the *L*s, then plucked a copy of *A Wrinkle in Time* off the shelf and handed it to Gabe. He read the back of the book cover slowly, nodding every now and again, and then opened it. When it looked like he might really be into the story, Bernetta selected a book for herself, *Something Wicked This Way Comes*. She leafed through it, but she couldn't help glancing over at Gabe every few seconds to see how much he was enjoying his book. He clucked his tongue at something, and she leaned over his shoulder to see what page he was on.

"It's good, right?" she asked him.

"Pretty good, yeah. It would make a good movie."

Bernetta rolled her eyes. "*Anyway,*" she said, "there was some trick or something you wanted to show me?"

"Oh, yeah." Gabe slid the book back onto the shelf. "Okay, first we have to find a mark."

"A mark?"

"Yeah, that means the victim, the guy we're going to con. Actually, you know, now that we're partners, I should probably teach you the lingo."

"What do you mean, the lingo?"

"You know, the way con artists talk to each other."

"Don't they just talk like everyone else?"

"No, they have all these cool words for everything. You'll like it. Okay, so there's the mark, right?"

"Right," Bernetta said, "the victim."

"Right. Then there's the roper. That's the guy who brings in the mark, who becomes friends with him and stuff, so he thinks the con is for real. They use ropers a lot in long cons."

"What's a long con?"

Gabe picked another book off the shelf and flipped through it. "It's a really big con, not like the stuff we're doing. It usually takes forever to set up, and there's tons of people involved—like in *The Sting*, there are all these guys in costumes and this fake gambling place and everything. It's always kind of crazy and really hard to pull off, but you can make a whole ton of money all at once. Sometimes the guys even fake their own deaths at the end. That's called the cackle-bladder."

"Um, ew," Bernetta said. "That's seriously disgust—"

Gabe put a hand on her arm and pointed to the register, where a large woman was purchasing a stack of books. She handed over a gift card, and the cashier rang up her purchase. As he handed back the card, the cashier told her, "Your remaining balance is one hundred thirty-five dollars and sixty-two cents." The woman put the card back in her wallet.

Gabe's eyes were wide as he turned to Bernetta. "Perfect," he told her. "This is perfect. I was going to try a bill switch, but gift cards are *gold*. Come on," he said, grabbing Bernetta's arm. "We gotta follow her."

Bernetta barely had time to squeeze her book back onto the shelf before they hustled their way out of the store, right on the heels of the woman with the large bag of books.

They scurried after her, trying to remain inconspicuous but still stepping on a few toes and nudging a few passersby here or there. Finally the woman came to a stop in the food court, heading to the back of the line at Salads and Ballads. Gabe led Bernetta to the pizza line at the next stand over.

"So, what are we doing exactly?" Bernetta asked Gabe as they inched forward in line.

"Buying lunch," Gabe replied. He scanned the tables. "Good," he said. "It's crowded."

They paid for their pizza, and Gabe short-changed himself a small profit. Then they wormed their way through the crowd, gripping their orange lunch trays. "Over there," Gabe said, pointing the way with his chin. He headed directly for the middle of the dining area, where the lady from the bookstore sat by herself at a table for four. Her bag of books was perched on one of the chairs. When they were about twenty feet from the table, Gabe yanked Bernetta behind a row of garbage cans and crouched down low. Bernetta followed suit. She didn't know what else to do.

"Okay, so here's the plan," Gabe whispered to her. "I'll do most of the talking. You just play along. And when the time comes, you snag her gift card. Sound good?"

"Um, what?" Bernetta almost upended her tray, and she grabbed her soda just in time. Gabe's plan did *not* sound good. "No way. I'm not going to steal her card. It's in her wallet. You saw her put it in there yourself. No way I could get it out of there even if I wanted to."

"You stole my watch right off my wrist without me even noticing," Gabe said. "Of course you can do it."

Bernetta shook her head. "You said people would be *handing* us stuff."

Gabe paused. "Okay," he said. "How about we make another bet?" Bernetta squinted an eye at him, but he continued. "You owe me ten dollars, right? Well, if I can't get that woman to hand you her wallet, then I owe *you* ten dollars. But if I *can* get her to give it to you, then you have to take that gift card. Just slip it out without her noticing. You can totally do it. You have lightning hands. And if you do that, then we'll be even. You won't owe me anything."

Bernetta raised her eyebrows. "You think you can get her to *give* me her wallet?" Gabe nodded. "She's going to put it right in my hands?" He nodded again.

Bernetta thought about it for a moment. There was absolutely no way Gabe could pull that off. And if he could, she definitely wanted to know how.

"Deal," she said at last.

Gabe just smiled and grabbed Bernetta's soda off her tray. "Excellent," he replied, and took a good long gulp.

They reached the table, and Gabe smiled at the lady, warm and convincing, just like Bernetta's father when he worked his close-up magic. "Hi," Gabe said to the woman, in an I'm-just-an-innocent-kid-so-don't-worry voice. "Mind if we share this table with you? It's pretty crowded."

A quick look around informed Bernetta that there were at least two other tables they could have sat at, but the woman didn't seem to notice.

"No problem," she said, shifting her bag of books to the floor. She glanced at them briefly, then went back to her salad, stabbing a tomato with her plastic fork.

Gabe plopped himself down right next to the lady, so Bernetta sat too, directly across from him. Gabe took a bite of his pizza, and so did Bernetta. He was acting pretty normal, Bernetta thought. He wasn't even paying attention to the woman. There was no way he was going to get her to hand Bernetta her wallet at this rate. Bernetta took a bite of her pizza and smiled at him across the table.

He smiled right back. "So," Gabe said to Bernetta. His voice was calm and easy. "Did you find out when your cousin is going to have the baby yet?"

"Um . . ." Bernetta raised an eyebrow. She only had two cousins, and they were both under ten. But she'd promised to play along, so she did her best. "Um, yeah, I don't know. Soon, though. Real soon. Any minute maybe. She could be having it right now."

"Oh, yeah?" He took a bite of his pizza. "Is it a boy or a girl?"

"Um, it's a girl, I think."

Gabe was opening his mouth to say something else when the woman next to him cut him off. "You know, my daughter just had a baby," she said. Her face was beaming with pride. "A little girl too." The lady turned to Bernetta. "Does your cousin have a name picked out yet?"

"Yeah, um . . ." Bernetta glanced at Gabe, but he just wiped his mouth with his napkin. No help at all. "I think they might name it Wallamina?"

"Oh." The lady's eyebrows shot up. "Well, that's certainly interesting."

Bernetta smiled, all teeth. "It's a family name," she explained.

"I see." The woman speared a cucumber and

popped it into her mouth.

"When did your daughter have her baby?" Gabe asked. Bernetta couldn't help wondering where this weird baby obsession of Gabe's had come from or how on earth it was going to help them get that gift card. Maybe Gabe just really liked babies.

The lady held her hand in front of her mouth to let them know she was still chewing. Once she had swallowed, she replied, "Just two weeks ago." She smiled wide. "It's her first. Angela Grace, isn't that a beautiful name? I'm flying out to see them all tomorrow."

Gabe smiled back. "I bet she's just adorable," he said.

"She is," the woman said. "Would you like to see a picture?"

"I'd love to!" Gabe replied. Bernetta squinted at him from behind her pizza. None of the boys at Mount Olive ever wanted to look at pictures of babies, she was pretty sure of that.

The woman pulled her wallet out of her purse and flipped through the pictures in the middle. "Here," she said, showing Gabe the photo on top. "That's Angela on the day she was born. She's something, isn't she?"

Gabe took the wallet for a closer look, and to

Bernetta's surprise the woman let him without blinking an eye. He studied the photo for several seconds and then handed it back. "She's really cute," he told the woman.

She held the photo close to her nose and sighed, still staring at it. "Isn't she, though?" She turned to Bernetta. "Would you like to see too?" she asked.

Bernetta sucked in a quick breath of air. "Oh, I—" she said, eyes darting in Gabe's direction. No way he pulled it off. No *way*. "I don't know, my hands are all greasy."

"Here, Jenny," Gabe said, his chocolate brown eyes sparkling. "Use my napkin."

"You really have to see her," the woman said, thrusting her wallet at Bernetta. "I may be biased, but I think she's simply the prettiest thing there is."

Bernetta cleared her throat and wiped her greasy fingers on Gabe's napkin. Then she took the wallet.

This was it, Bernetta thought, the wallet clenched in her hands. Gabe had done his part, and she'd promised she'd take the gift card, so she had to do it. Bernetta Wallflower was no welsher. And she did have lightning fingers. But the woman still had her eyes firmly planted on the wallet, smiling down at the photo inside.

Until Gabe dropped his fork. It flipped right off his tray, landing on the floor with a soft clank, and the woman's gaze went with it.

In the split second that the woman looked away, Bernetta slid her thumb into the slit of the wallet and slipped out the bookstore gift card. It was stowed safely in her pocket before the woman even turned back around.

"She's beautiful," Bernetta told the woman as she returned the wallet.

"I think so anyway," the lady replied. She took one last glance at the photo and then put the wallet back in her purse. "I guess I'm just a doting grandmother."

After the woman had finished her salad and was safely out of view, Bernetta handed the gift card over to Gabe.

"See?" he told her. "I told you you could do it! You're like the Artful Dodger in *Oliver Twist*."

Bernetta shrugged. "I guess. How did you know she'd show us her baby photos?"

"I saw her at the bookstore," Gabe replied. "She was buying a whole stack of baby books. *Goodnight Moon*, *Pat the Bunny*, everything. New grandmas always have pictures. And they *always* want to show them to you." He put the card in his pocket. "I'm good at reading people, and you have killer hands. We're the perfect team. I told you, right?"

Well, Bernetta thought, Gabe certainly was good at reading people, that was true enough. He'd figured out that new grandmother in a heartbeat. More than that, he'd figured Bernetta out too. Hadn't he been convinced all along that she'd become his partner? And Bernetta had simply thought he was crazy. But Gabe, it turned out, had read her like a book. Was Bernetta really the type of girl who stole things from innocent people? Gabe seemed to think she was. And Bernetta had to admit that she was having much more fun being the girl Gabe thought she was than she'd been having as the falsely accused grounded-for-the-summer cheater. Maybe Gabe was right about her. Maybe this was who she'd been all along.

She took the last sip of her soda and set her cup down on her tray. "So what do we do now?" she asked.

Gabe picked up the cup, popped off the lid, and tilted it into his mouth. He crunched on an ice cube and smiled at her. "Let's go see if they changed cashiers at the bookstore yet," he said. "I have a plan. You're going to love it."

Once they were back inside the bookstore, Gabe and Bernetta ducked behind the arts and entertainment section. "Good," Gabe said to Bernetta, "there's a new girl at the register. Now we can turn the gift card into cash."

"Why does it matter if there's someone new at the register?" Bernetta asked.

"It's just safer," Gabe replied. "This way no one will recognize us. Or remember the card. Come on, help me look. We have to find someone to let us pay for their books."

Bernetta and Gabe scanned the aisles together, standing side by side with their noses buried inside a large book on film criticism.

"What about that guy?" Bernetta asked, pointing to a man about her father's age approaching the register. "He looks pretty nice. I bet he'd help us out."

"Probably," Gabe said. "But he's only getting one book. And it's a paperback. We should wait for someone with a big stack, so we can make more in one go."

"Oh. Okay." Bernetta was still trying to get a grasp of this whole *reading people* thing. There was a lot to keep track of. "What about that lady over there? The one in the blue dress."

Gabe looked to where Bernetta was tilting her chin. "No way," he said. "Look what section she's in."

Bernetta read the sign above the lady's head: TRUE CRIME. "So?"

"She could be a cop," Gabe said. "Or a law student or something. That could get tricky."

"Oh," Bernetta said with a gulp.

"I found someone," he said, and he snapped the book closed. "That girl right over there. She's got a *ton* of books. Come on."

The girl may have had a ton of books, Bernetta thought as she followed Gabe to the register, but she also didn't look like someone to mess with. She had straight blond hair pulled into a no-nonsense ponytail, and she looked just a few years younger than Elsa. Her black backpack was covered in tiny pins and patches from bands that Bernetta was not nearly cool enough to have heard of.

Gabe tapped the girl on the shoulder just as she was getting in line behind an old man with a cane.

The blond girl turned around. "Yeah?" she said, her eyebrow already raised in annoyance.

"Oh," Gabe said, and Bernetta could tell that he

was a little startled at the girl's response. Bernetta stayed off to the side, a few feet to Gabe's right, to watch and learn.

Gabe cleared his throat. "I was just wondering if I could buy those books for you with this gift card," he said, holding out the card. "Then you could give me the money you would have spent."

The blond-haired girl tilted her head and offered Gabe a phony smile, like he was the ugliest boy in school, asking to take her to the winter formal. Bernetta instantly disliked her. "Yeah," the girl said, her head cocked to the side, "I don't really want to do that. Thanks, though." And she spun back around, her long blond ponytail swishing in Gabe's face as she turned.

Gabe tapped her on the shoulder. "Are you sure you don't—"

"Yep," she said without looking in Gabe's direction. "I'm sure."

Gabe frowned at Bernetta and was making to walk away when Bernetta got a good look at one of the patches on the girl's backpack: Wayland High Junior Varsity Cheerleading.

Bernetta took a deep breath and stepped toward the girl. Then, as Gabe shot her a quizzical glance, she tapped the girl's shoulder.

"What?" the girl demanded before she'd even turned around.

Bernetta didn't back down. "Hi," she said. "Um, hi, I just . . ." Bernetta had a fraction of a second before she lost the girl for good, she could tell. "I'm trying to go to cheer camp," she said quickly.

The blond girl turned back to Bernetta, sucking in her cheeks as she studied her up and down. "You cheer?" she asked.

"Um, yeah," Bernetta said. "Well, I want to anyway. But cheerleading camp starts in two weeks, and my parents can't afford it, so I asked my grandma for money for my birthday, but instead she gave me this card, 'cause she says I should read more." Bernetta felt like her dad for a moment, dancing nimbly around the stage just before he thrust out his wand for the big reveal. "Anyway, my brother here"—she motioned to Gabe—"was just trying to help me out, but sorry if we bugged you." And she grabbed Gabe by the elbow and pulled him, stumbling, toward the exit. She had no idea if that was the right thing to do, but Gabe's way hadn't worked either, so she figured, why not?

They were almost out the door when—

"Hey, wait up!" the blond girl called out.

Bernetta and Gabe turned. The girl had her head cocked to the side again, but this time she didn't look quite so intimidating.

"You going into eighth?" she asked Bernetta.

"Yep," Bernetta lied.

The blond girl finally smiled. "That's when I started too. What school do you go to?"

"Kingsfield Middle." Another lie. That was Ashley's old school. Mount Olive didn't have cheer-leading. Maybe the blond girl wouldn't know that, but Bernetta didn't want to take any chances.

"Kingsfield!" the blond girl shrieked. "Really? That's where I went too. Who'd you have for home-room last year?"

Shoot.

Bernetta thought fast. "Mrs. Vincent." That was her homeroom teacher at Mount Olive. "I think she's new. She's kind of strict, but not too bad."

"Oh." The blond girl nodded. "I had Mr. Prolanski." She rolled her eyes, and Bernetta did too.

"Blech," she said. "My friend Stephanie had him, and she said he was *horrible*."

"Yeah. He was pretty awful."

The blond girl's books came to $58.27, but she gave Bernetta an even sixty.

"Good luck at cheer camp!" she called as she headed out of the store.

"Thanks!" Bernetta shouted back.

At her side Gabe was looking at her and nodding, a grin stretched across his face. "Cheer camp, huh?" he said. "Not bad. You're a regular Bonnie Parker." Bernetta could feel herself blushing. "Yeah." He nodded again. "Not bad at all."

12

> **☞transformation** *n:* an illusion in which one object becomes another

In only one day Bernetta and Gabe managed to make a bucketload of money. They'd had one close scrape when a cashier in a department store had tried to call his manager over while Gabe was attempting a shortchange, but Gabe had been pretty convincing when he told the guy he'd just been confused math-wise about the change, and they made it out of the store without arousing further suspicion. Once they'd split the day's take, Bernetta left the mall with $183.71 stowed safely inside her backpack.

Now she sat at the dinner table and took up a forkful of chicken, trying to figure out the best way to answer her family's questions.

"So how was your day?" her mother asked.

Bernetta swallowed. "Good," she replied. "Really good."

Her father was busy buttering a roll. "How are the kids?"

Bernetta took another giant bite and got away with a mere nod in response. A part of her wished she could tell her family what she'd *really* been up to. Because she *had* had a good day; that part hadn't been a lie at all. It was amazing the way she'd learned to read people in just a few hours—figure out which cashiers were nice and which ones were surly, just by the way they tapped their fingers on the counter or stuck a pen behind an ear.

But those were obviously skills she was going to have to keep to herself.

"So, Elsa," their father said, "what time are you leaving for volleyball camp tomorrow?"

"Really early," she said as she scooped rice onto her fork. "Before dawn, I think."

Bernetta set her fork down. "Camp starts tomorrow?" she asked.

"Yeah," Elsa replied. "It's a really long drive, too. I'll be gone before you get up. And I'm not even close to packed, either."

"Well, make sure you get enough rest for your drive tomorrow," their mother said. "Colin, eat your broccoli, please."

"Beep beep boop beep," Colin replied.

"What was that?" Bernetta's father asked.

"I'm an alien," Colin explained. "I can only speak in alienese. I mean, beep beep bang."

Bernetta wasn't really listening. How could she possibly have forgotten that Elsa's camp started tomorrow? This wasn't fair at all. It was the last summer before Elsa left for college, and she was spending practically all of it at *volleyball camp*. Once Elsa left in the fall, that would be it. Things would be permanently different in the Wallflower family. No Elsa at the dinner table, no big sister to practice new magic tricks on, no one to paint her toenails with when life was particularly upsetting.

Bernetta took a bite of rice, but the grains felt dry on her tongue.

"So, Bernetta," her mom said, "tell us what kinds of things you do with the kids while the parents are working."

Bernetta tried to make her bite of rice last as long as possible, but eventually she had to stop chewing.

"Oh, you know," she said, "just regular kid stuff."

Elsa folded her napkin and set it on the table. "Well, I think I better get packing," she said, pushing back her chair and taking her plate to the sink. "Netta, if you want, we can paint our toes one last time before I leave."

Bernetta took up another forkful of broccoli. "Yeah," she said. "Sure. I'd like that."

"All right, just knock on my door before you go to sleep." She rinsed her plate and left the kitchen.

Bernetta was taking a drink of water when Colin lunged at her, his fingers wiggling in her face. *"Eek!"* he cried.

Bernetta swallowed. "What was *that* about, Colander?"

"Aren't you gonna get all scared and scream, Bernie?" he asked. "I'm an alien! I mean, eek ack woo ha-ha."

Bernetta bit her lip, but she couldn't stop smiling. "Oh," she said. "Yeah, Coliseum, you're really scary. I mean, bim bam beeple snartz."

═══════

After dinner was over and the dishes were washed and dried, Bernetta went up to Elsa's room to keep her company while she packed. Bernetta sat on the bed with her fingers woven between her toes while Elsa squatted on the floor in front of her duffel bag, folding T-shirts.

"Do you really have to go to camp?" Bernetta asked as Elsa tucked a stack of shirts neatly inside the bag. "I mean, you don't really *need* to, right? You already know how to play volleyball. You're pretty good at it."

"Not compared to all those college girls. You should have seen them, Netta. I told you about that game Dad and I went to when we were visiting. I'm serious, those girls are on a whole different level. They're practically professionals."

"Still," Bernetta said, scratching the underside of her foot, "you don't want to be gone the whole summer. Aren't you going to be bored out of your mind, playing volleyball all day long? And they're going to make you do all those drills, and you *hate* drills."

Elsa shook her head as she began folding shorts, but she was smiling. "And what would I do here all summer, hmm?"

Bernetta shrugged. "I don't know. Play cards with Colin? He's getting really good at war. Plus, you know"—she hooked her pinkie fingers around her little toes—"you could hang out with me. It's our last summer together before you go to college."

"That's true," Elsa said, shoving her neat stack of T-shirts into a corner to make room for the shorts. "But even if I *was* here, I'd hardly get to see you anyway, now that you're babysitting so much."

"Yeah, I guess," Bernetta said with a sigh.

Elsa leaned back on her heels and looked up. "What was that giant sigh about, Netta?"

Bernetta puffed out her cheeks and tried to put the thoughts swirling around in her brain into words. "It's just—you're *leaving*, right? You'll be in a whole different state next year, and I won't get to talk to you anymore."

"Netta, what are you talking about? We'll talk all the time. There's this nifty new invention, you know, called the telephone?"

Bernetta rolled her eyes. "But I won't *see* you ever."

"I'll be home for Thanksgiving."

"That's practically a million years away!" Bernetta cried. "And what if you make tons of cool new college friends, and get a *boyfriend*, and pierce your nose or something? Then you'll come home and I won't even recognize you."

Elsa just laughed. "Now you sound like Dad," she said.

"But aren't you worried?" Bernetta asked. "I mean, you don't even know anyone there and you'll have to live in a dorm room, with strangers. What if you hate your roommate? What if the food is awful, or you get lost somewhere, or—or anything?"

Elsa shook her head as she began to roll up pairs of socks. "I guess I'm just excited, that's all," she said. "I mean, I've gone to the same school for thirteen years and lived in the same house for eighteen. I guess I'm ready for a change."

Bernetta frowned. *Mount Olive's not so bad,* she thought. *We're not so bad either.* But she didn't say it.

Elsa stood up and headed over to the dresser. "Let's do our nails. I need a break."

"Okay," Bernetta said. She ran a finger over her blue toenail polish, already chipped in two places after only three days. Maybe she was being a tad over-dramatic about the whole college thing. It would all work out. Isn't that what their mom always said?

"What color?" Elsa asked her, shifting through the contents of her top drawer.

Bernetta bit her lip and thought about it. "Um, Rustic Red, I think."

"Knew it!" Elsa cried. She turned around with a

smile and stretched out her hand toward Bernetta. She was already clasping a bottle of burgundy-colored polish.

Bernetta frowned. "How'd you know I was going to pick that one?" she asked.

"Because I know you, Netta," Elsa answered as she produced the nail polish remover and cotton balls. "You always pick the same colors." She plopped down on the bed. "Rustic Red when you're worried about something, Blueberry Bramble when you're angry, and Tangerine Delicious when you have good news." She unscrewed the lid of the polish remover. "Same old Netta. Here, give me your foot."

Bernetta wrinkled her forehead and slowly wrapped her arms around her legs.

"Netta?" Elsa asked. "Is something wrong?"

Same old Netta? Is that what Elsa thought of her? Elsa could go off to camp and then move to a different state and forget all about everything back at home, and Bernetta was just supposed to stick around and take it? Same old Netta? "Actually," Bernetta said softly, "I think I'm kind of tired. All that babysitting, you know?"

Elsa frowned. "Oh." She put the cap back on the bottle. "Okay. If you're sure."

"Yeah. Anyway, good night, I guess. Have fun at camp."

They both stood up then and hugged, but it was forced, like they'd never hugged before and didn't know who should lean in which direction and how long they should stay hugging before they broke apart.

As Bernetta headed for the door, Elsa said, "Netta?" Bernetta turned. "You sure you're okay?"

"Yeah," Bernetta said.

"Well, I'll miss you, you know?"

Bernetta nodded, her chin scrunched up tight. "I'll miss you too," she said. And she headed off to her room.

—————

Thirty minutes later Bernetta was in her pajamas, bundled under her covers with her old worn copy of *A Wrinkle in Time* resting against her knees. But she wasn't enjoying the story as much as she usually did. It didn't even taste as good.

There was a knock on the door, and her father appeared in the doorway.

"Hey, Bernie," he said. "Can I come in for a sec? I have a trick I've been wanting to show you."

She snapped her book shut. "Sure."

He sat down on the edge of her bed and pulled out

a quarter. He held it up with his left hand, then reached across and grabbed it with his right. He closed his right hand into a fist and pointed to it with his left. Then he opened his right hand slowly, one finger at a time.

The quarter had vanished.

Bernetta smiled at him, her anger at Elsa melting away. "Nice."

"Where do you think the quarter went?" he asked her.

She thought about it. "Still in your left hand?"

He raised an eyebrow and smiled. "Very astute, Bernie. Yep, I never grabbed it. That's the French Drop. It's the oldest trick in the book, practically, but anyone will fall for it if you pull it off correctly. People are practically dying to fall for it, really."

"Yeah?"

"See, once you bring your right hand over to your left one, your audience is expecting you to transfer that quarter. They've got no reason to think you'd do anything else. That is, unless you give them some reason, like staring at your left hand when they think the coin's moved on to your right. Never look at the wrong hand, Bernie. That'll ruin your trick in a heartbeat." He handed her the quarter. "You want to try it?"

Bernetta studied the quarter a moment and then tried the trick, just as her father had showed her. Left hand, quarter. Right hand, sweep and close.

"Bernie!" her dad cried. "That was amazing! Almost perfect. I've never seen anyone pick it up so quickly. You really are a natural. I couldn't believe that trick you pulled the other night at the club."

"Yeah?" Bernetta smiled.

"Bram's still talking about it."

Bernetta laughed.

"Listen," her father told her, "I know your mother and I agreed that you should take a break from the club this summer, but I really think you should keep practicing your magic, regardless. You have a real talent. And who knows? When the school year starts back up again, we just might be able to work you into more of the show."

Bernetta clapped her hands. "Really? Are you serious, Dad?"

"Absolutely. If you keep practicing."

She gave him a hug, and then he wished her good night. "Did you say good-bye to your sister?" he asked on his way to the door. "You probably won't see her tomorrow."

"Mmm-hmm," Bernetta replied, whacking her pillow into its fluffiest position.

After her father had closed the door behind him, Bernetta took up the coin again and felt the weight of it in her left hand. She studied it there. *Never look at the wrong hand,* her father had said. Strange, Bernetta thought, but what her father had taught her that evening was so similar to what Gabe had shown her that afternoon. Distraction, making others look only where you want them to. She set the quarter down on her bed and rustled through her backpack until she found a ten-dollar bill. Then, with her stuffed pink pig as a cashier, she practiced the moves of the short-change over and over, until she knew she had it down better than even Gabe did.

When the clock read 10:02 and her yawns were starting to stretch her jaw farther and farther down, Bernetta stuffed the bills from her shortchange practice into her top desk drawer. As she snuggled under her covers for a good night's sleep, the quarter for the French Drop rolled off her bedspread and onto the floor with a soft clunk, but Bernetta didn't bother to pick it up. It had been a long day, and she was, at last, ready to go to sleep.

───────

When Bernetta woke up the next morning, she found a note on top of her desk.

> *Dear Netta,*
>
> > *Thought you might want to use this while I was gone. Have a great summer! I'll see you in five weeks.*
>
> > > > *Love,*
> > > > *Elsa*

Next to the note was a half-empty bottle of Rustic Red nail polish.

Bernetta picked up the bottle and stared at it for a moment. Then, very slowly, she crossed the room and dumped the bottle in the trash can.

Elsa didn't know everything about her, Bernetta realized. Not even close. Maybe her sister was going off to college soon, but she wasn't the only one doing new things. She wasn't the only one who was changing.

As Bernetta passed her dresser, she noticed last night's quarter on the floor, next to her bed. She scooped it up and added it to her Mount Olive fund in the desk drawer. Every little bit helped.

13

> **short card** *n*: a card that has been slightly shortened, making it easy to locate within a deck of otherwise unaltered cards

With each day that passed, Bernetta found that she was getting better and better at pulling cons. She and Gabe made excellent partners—he'd been completely right about that. He was a whiz at reading people, and she wasn't too shabby either. She had those lightning hands, and he had a way of turning his voice silky smooth, so that people couldn't help trusting him. Gabe didn't want to stay in one location too long, so they'd spend a couple of days at the Championship Mall and then switch to the movie theater or the strip mall across town. A few times they even took the bus to the pier twenty minutes away, where there were loads of tourists just waiting to hand them their money. No matter who had raked in the most money that day, they always split the take evenly when they parted ways for the evening—exactly fifty-fifty. By early July, just three and a half weeks after Bernetta had joined forces with Gabe, she'd made over a fourth of her tuition money. Mount Olive was waiting for her with open arms.

One Thursday night during dinner Bernetta was busy composing the speech she'd make to Ashley Johansson the day she waltzed back into school. She couldn't decide if it should begin with "So who's the idiot *now*?" or the slightly more humble "I guess you thought you'd gotten rid of me for good, huh?" She was trying to imagine the look on Ashley's face—mostly shock, probably, with a good mix of scorn and confusion—when Colin poked her in the side with a spoon.

"BernieBernieBernie, did you go to Saturn?"

"Huh?"

Their father laughed and twirled his spaghetti on his fork. "I think he's wondering if your mind's in outer space."

"Oh." Bernetta wiped a glob of sauce she'd just noticed on her elbow. "No, I was just thinking."

"Well," her mother said as she poured dressing on

her salad, "your father and I were just talking about your babysitting money."

Bernetta's head shot up. "Oh?"

"Yes. I opened up a savings account for you this afternoon. I think it's best if you put the money the Nortons have been giving you in the bank. That way you can earn a little interest off it too—won't that be nice?"

Bernetta nodded. "Um, yeah. Thanks, Mom."

"Tomorrow, when you're done babysitting, I'll take you to make your first deposit, all right? After that you can go yourself after the Nortons pay you each week. How does that sound?"

"Great." She took a slurp of spaghetti, a noodle worming its way up her chin.

The phone rang in the living room, and Bernetta's mom left the table to answer it.

"Hey, Bernie!" Colin called out suddenly. He held up his left hand, which was sporting a flowery oven mitt. "Give me two!" he shouted.

"What?" Bernetta asked.

"Give me *two*," Colin repeated. He looked at her like she was an idiot and pointed to the oven mitt. "Like, give me *five*. But it looks like I only got two fingers."

Bernetta rolled her eyes. "Brilliant, Colinization."

"Really? You think I'm brilliant?"

"Yes. You're a genius."

"Nah," Colin said, scratching his head with his oven mitt hand. "I don't even have a bottle."

"*What?*" Bernetta said.

Their dad put his hand in front of his mouth and stage-whispered, "He thinks you said *genie*."

"Oh."

Bernetta's mother walked back into the kitchen then and let out a puff of air as she sat down at the table. "I have to go in to school tomorrow morning," she told everyone. "Mrs. Eddleman was supposed to administer the proficiency tests to the new special ed students, but apparently she's come down with the flu."

"Is she okay?" Bernetta asked.

"Is she barfing all over everywhere?" Colin said.

"She'll be fine," their mother replied. "But Herbert, do you think you can take Colin to rehearsal with you tomorrow?"

"I'd love to," he said. "Only I'm not going to rehearsal tomorrow. Roger's buying a new illusion from a seller out in Crestlake, and he asked me to go with him."

Bernetta's mother twisted her spaghetti around on her plate. "I see. Well, Bernetta, maybe you could take him with you to the Nortons' house then?"

Bernetta accidentally bit her tongue instead of her food. "No!" she cried. She stuck her tongue out, rubbing it between her fingers. "I meem—" She took her fingers out of her mouth and tried again. "I mean, um, I don't think the Nortons would really—"

"I'm sure they'd understand," her mother said. "I'll call them." She got up and walked back toward the phone. "Where did you put their number, sweetie?"

"Mom, wait!" Bernetta cried, leaping out of her chair. "Um, I'll call them."

Bernetta's mother nodded. "Okay."

———

Bernetta held the phone tight to her ear, her mother lurking at her elbow. "No, really, Mrs. Norton, that's okay," Bernetta said into the receiver. "Don't worry about it at all."

"And this Tuesday is Family Fun Night!" the robotic voice on the other end informed her. "Tickets for parents and children are only four dollars each for the six-P.M. screening of *Little Choo Choo's Big Achoo*."

"No, that's fine," Bernetta said. "If Colin really

can't come over tomorrow, I'm sure my mom can drop him off at a friend's house or something."

Bernetta's mother shook her head. "No," she said. "Zack's family is at the Grand Canyon, and the Cartwrights have company this week." She reached for the phone. "Here, let me talk to her."

Bernetta coughed. "Um, what?" she said into the receiver. "What's that, Mrs. Norton?" Bernetta held her hand over the mouthpiece and turned to her mom. "She's talking to her husband. I think she might be changing her mind."

"Oh, good."

A minute later, after listening to all the listings for *A Long, Long Way to Jupiter*, Bernetta hung up the phone and informed her parents that the Nortons had agreed to have Colin over for the day. She couldn't think of anything else to say.

"Oh, good," Colin said. "I want to play board games with Hank. Board games with lots of pieces."

Bernetta didn't even have the strength to muster up a sigh. Tomorrow was going to be one interesting day.

━━━━━━

Early the next morning Bernetta sat on the floor of her room, tying her shoelaces and thinking. She'd been up thinking most of the night, actually. But so far she hadn't come up with a way around her predicament. She'd promised Gabe that she'd meet him at the pier that morning, and she desperately wanted to go. She hated the thought of Gabe stuck out there all morning, waiting for her, wondering why she hadn't shown up.

But then there was Colin. Her little brother might not be the brightest star in the cosmos, but he wasn't a moron either, and when she failed to take him to Hank and Yolanda's house, he was going to figure out that something was up. And then he was going to tell that *something* to their parents.

There was a knock on her bedroom door.

"Yeah?"

The door opened. "Hey, sweetie." It was her mother. "Thank you again for taking Colin with you this morning. Are you sure you don't need a ride over there?"

"Nah. Colin likes walking."

"He does. Okay, I wanted to give you the information for your savings account, so you can make your deposit this afternoon. I would go with you, but I'll probably be at school pretty late. Don't forget, all right?"

"I won't."

After Bernetta's mother had explained how to

deposit the money and gone back downstairs to make sure Colin ate his breakfast, Bernetta opened her desk drawer and took out all her precious Mount Olive money. She wrapped the bills in three layers of Kleenex, pressed the wad between the pages of her well-chewed copy of *Dune*, and wrapped the whole thing with a rubber band. Then she placed the book carefully at the bottom of her backpack and covered it with a sweatshirt. If she had to carry her entire school fund all the way to the bank, she was going to make sure it was safe and secure.

Bernetta walked downstairs and found Colin eating scrambled eggs at the kitchen table. He was wearing his last year's Halloween costume, cape and all, but his fangs seemed to be getting in the way as he chewed.

"Colobus Monkey," Bernetta said, grabbing a piece of toast their mother had left and taking a seat at the table, "you are not wearing that outside."

"Yes, I am," he said. "And my name's not Colobus Monkey. It's Dracula."

"No way," Bernetta said. "No way am I taking you all over town looking like—"

"Hey, Bernie!" he cried suddenly, pulling the fangs out of his mouth. "Wanna see something really scary?"

He set the fangs on her plate. They were covered in egg bits and drool.

Bernetta wrinkled her nose. "Ew!" she said. "That's *gross*, not scary."

Colin rolled his eyes. "That's 'cause I'm not done yet. Duh." He grabbed the ketchup bottle off the table and took aim at the fangs. "They need blood. Then they'll be scary."

"Colin . . ."

The ketchup splattered onto Bernetta's plate.

"See?" Colin asked. "Spooky, huh?" And he popped the ketchupy fangs back into his mouth.

Bernetta tried not to gag on her toast as their mother bustled into the room, gathering odds and ends into her purse. "You two better get going," she said, checking her watch. "You don't want to be late for the Nortons."

"Right," Bernetta said, taking her plate full of ketchup to the sink. "Come on, Dracula. I guess we should go."

"Yay!" Colin cried, jumping out of his chair, his cape swishing behind him. "Dracula loves board games!"

Bernetta slid her backpack onto her shoulders and tightened the straps.

"Have fun!" their mom said, with a peck on the forehead for each child.

"We will!" Colin told her.

Bernetta wasn't so sure.

———

"So, Colin," Bernetta said as they set off walking. The going was pretty slow because Colin kept tripping on his Dracula cape, and he stopped every three seconds to pick up rocks. "How about we don't actually go to the Nortons' house today? What if we went somewhere else? Like, um, the pier?"

Colin bent down to pick up another rock. "But I thought you had to babysit Hank and Yoyo today."

"Um, well, normally I do, but today . . ." Bernetta watched as Colin attempted to cram yet another rock in his pocket. There must have been ten in there already. "Colin, what are you doing?"

"I'm collecting all the gray ones."

"Oh. Okay. Um, anyway . . . I think today Hank's not feeling so good. He's kind of sick actually. So I don't have to babysit. So the two of us should just take the bus to the pier instead. What do you think of that? We can go on the Ferris wheel."

Colin stood and held up a rock to Bernetta's nose.

"Bernie, you think this is a baby rock or a grown-up grandma one? I have five babies already, so I need some grandmas."

By the time they reached the bus stop three blocks away, Colin's pockets were bulging with rocks, and he didn't seem to care one smidge about imaginary Hank and invisible Yolanda. So they waited together while Colin examined his new rock collection, and when the bus arrived, Bernetta offered the driver a handful of quarters and they climbed on board. Colin spent the full twenty minutes balancing rocks on Bernetta's knees, telling her each stone's life story.

"This one," he told Bernetta, "is named Blubber-Baby Teeny-Meany Rock Guy. He's a tightrope walker in the circus. He's really really good too, and he only falls over sometimes. His pet elephant has the measles, though. And *this* one is Mrs. Waffle House. She works at the bank, catching bad guys who try to rob the money. She has nineteen kids, and her uncle is an astronaut. This one's name is Norm, and he eats soap."

When the bus lurched to a stop, Bernetta helped Colin scoop the rocks back into his pockets, and then she took his hand and led him down the bus steps, holding up the edge of his cape so he wouldn't trip on it.

The pier was one of Bernetta's favorite places in the world. It smelled like fish and salt water and sweat and sunscreen, and everywhere you looked, there were kids racing around with giant orange stuffed animals or pink cotton candy. When Bernetta was eight and Elsa was fourteen, Elsa had convinced their parents that they could go all by themselves, and they'd spent the whole day, just the two of them, eating hot dogs and riding the Ferris wheel and playing games and trying on hundreds of pairs of sunglasses. The pier was the perfect place for a sisters-only day.

It was also, Bernetta had discovered that summer, a pretty good place to be a con artist.

Bernetta spotted Gabe in front of the Taco Hut, right where he'd said he'd be, and she led Colin over. They walked across the swollen slats of the boardwalk, and Bernetta waved in Gabe's direction. Today his yellow T-shirt simply read I'M BATMAN.

"Hey," he said to Bernetta once they'd reached him. He smiled at Colin. "Hey, Boy Wonder. What's with the cape?"

"I'm Dracula," Colin said.

"He's my brother," Bernetta told him.

"I see."

Colin squinted up at Gabe. "Are you Hank?" he asked. He tugged on Bernetta's hand. "He's really big for a six-year-old. Tell him not to cough on me."

"Huh?" Bernetta asked.

"You said he was sick," Colin replied. He took his fangs out of his mouth and stuck them in his pocket. "Dracula hates getting sick. Can we play the games, Bernie Bernie? I wanna play the one with all the stuff you can knock over."

"Um . . ." Bernetta looked from Colin to Gabe and back again. "Actually," she said, "I think that's a great idea. Let's go."

As they headed over to the row of boardwalk games, Bernetta whispered to Gabe, "I had to bring him. Sorry. I would've called and canceled, but I didn't have your phone number." Bernetta sucked in her breath. She hoped Gabe didn't think she'd said that because she was trying to get him to give her his phone number. She tried to figure out a way to fix what she'd said, but before she could think of anything, they'd reached the games, and Colin was tugging on her arm again.

"That one, Bernie Bernie!" he squealed. "That one with the clown heads. Dracula *loves* knocking over clown heads!" He hopped up and down on one foot as Bernetta wrestled a few dollar bills out of her book-and-tissue-safe. She handed two to the man behind the booth, who gave Colin five softballs.

"You know what to do, kid?" the man asked Colin.

"Uh-huh," Colin said. "I whack all the clown heads."

"You got it," the man replied, and Colin began to throw.

"So?" Gabe said as they watched Colin try to take out the clowns. "Why are you carrying around so much money, anyway?"

"What?" Bernetta asked, clutching the straps on her backpack. "What do you mean?"

"I saw when you were getting money for Colin. You have a giant stash in your backpack. That's not really safe, you know, carrying around so much cash like that."

Bernetta watched as Colin's third ball finally took down a clown. "I know, but my mom's making me deposit all my school money in the bank, so I don't really have a choice. Hey, Colin hit another one! He's pretty good!"

"*All* your money?" Gabe asked.

"Yeah."

He frowned. "Well, maybe you shouldn't check to make sure your bag's zipped up all the time. It's a dead giveaway there's something valuable in there. Someone could steal it from you."

"What? That's crazy. No one's going to steal it. No one but you would even notice—"

"You're pulling on those straps so hard, your knuckles are white," Gabe told her. "Trust me, people notice stuff like that."

Bernetta loosened her grip on her backpack.

"Bernie Bernie!" Colin shouted. "I only hit two of the ugly clowns, and the man says I have to hit three or he won't give me a prize, even though I'm Dracula and I could eat him with my fangs."

Gabe laughed. "Don't worry, buddy," he told Colin, "I'll help you out." He dug in his pocket and pulled out two dollars, handing them to the man behind the booth. "I wouldn't want your brother to have to eat anyone," he said to Bernetta.

As Gabe took a stab at the clown game, and Colin did his best to frighten passing babies in strollers by showing off his fangs, Bernetta wondered if this was what it was like to be on a date. Down at the pier on a sunny summer day with a boy with chocolate brown eyes who was trying desperately to win a stuffed animal and impress you. Or impress your little brother. But close enough.

"I'm sorry Colin ruined our plans today," she told Gabe. "But I guess we can just, you know, hang out for a while. Colin will like that. I think he likes you. And then we can go back to normal on Monday."

Gabe tossed another ball, but he missed by a mile. "What do you mean, he ruined our plans? You don't want to work today?"

"Well, yeah, but I have to watch Colin."

Gabe threw another softball. Zero for three. "So? He could help us. I bet he'd be really good."

"Um—*what*?" Bernetta said. "You want him to work with us?" She watched Colin terrorizing toddlers. "I don't think that's a good idea. I mean, he's only six. It might scar him for life."

Gabe finally managed to hit a clown. "Yeah, but what if he didn't even know he was in on it?"

"I don't know . . ." Bernetta tugged on her backpack straps, but then noticed Gabe raising an eyebrow at her and let go.

"I think it would be perfect," Gabe said. "He's cute and little, so no one would suspect a thing. I know this really great con we could do, from *Paper Moon*." He threw the last two balls at once. Miss and miss. No prize. "Your brother likes ice cream, right?"

Bernetta thought about it. "You swear he won't know what we're doing?" Gabe nodded. "And there's no way we can get caught?" He shook his head no. Bernetta looked over at Colin. He seemed so happy. "All right," she said. "We're in."

"Cool," Gabe said. He checked his watch. "Why don't you guys play games for a little bit longer? I have to make a quick phone call. I'll be back in five minutes, and then I'll explain the plan. How's that?"

"Okay," Bernetta said, "see you in five."

14

[☞ **disappearance** *n:* an illusion in which a person or object vanishes]

Forty minutes later, after Gabe had explained his plan to Bernetta in full and had finally succeeded in winning Colin a blue stuffed whale, they left the game area.

"You feel like ice cream?" Bernetta asked Colin as they walked down the boardwalk.

Colin was busy trying to fit his Dracula fangs into the whale's stitched mouth. "Uh-huh. I *love* ice cream. Bernie Bernie, Dracula had a whale, right?"

"Of course he did."

"Good."

Colin skipped a few feet ahead, his whale clutched securely against his chest, then turned around and proceeded to walk backward, shouting out, "Make way for Dracula!" as he crashed into people.

"So," Bernetta said to Gabe as they walked, "this con, it's from a movie, you said?"

"*Paper Moon*, yeah. You seen it?"

She shook her head. "Nope."

"You should. It's really good."

It had been almost four weeks since Bernetta and Gabe had been working together, but Bernetta still didn't feel she knew how to have a *conversation* with him. What were you supposed to talk about on an almost date? Elsa would know, but she wasn't around, was she?

They walked past the Ferris wheel, with its calliope music and line of kids squealing happily. Bernetta tried desperately to think of something that Gabe would want to talk about. "So, um, is that your favorite movie?"

"Huh?" Gabe seemed to be lost in thought, but he snapped out of it quickly. "*Paper Moon*? No. I mean, it's good, but it's not my favorite."

"So what is?"

Up ahead of them, Colin crashed backward into a bench, but he got up just fine and waved and smiled before he began his backward walking again.

"Well . . ." Gabe thought about it. "Probably my favorite is *Bait and Switch*."

"Oh," Bernetta said. "I've never seen it." Why hadn't she ever seen any of the movies he liked?

"Yeah," Gabe replied, sticking his hands in his pockets. "Most people haven't. Actually, it's not even that good. I just like it because my uncle's in it."

"Really? Your uncle's in a movie? Is he an actor?"

Gabe grinned. "Yeah. Well, he's sort of an actor. He used to live in Hollywood and everything, but he moved back here a couple years ago 'cause he hardly got any gigs. That means acting jobs." Bernetta nodded. "He's always saying he's going to go back, though, take another stab at it. *Bait and Switch* is pretty cool. You should see it. The scene my uncle's in, he plays this waiter. And one of the bad guys is sitting in this booth at the restaurant, right? And my uncle serves him coffee. And then the guy *dies*. It's poison coffee." Bernetta laughed. "Uncle Kevin only had three lines, but it was still cool."

Gabe was looking at her then, giving her a good, serious gaze as they strolled down the boardwalk. He seemed to be thinking pretty hard about something. Bernetta wasn't positive, but she thought that maybe, just maybe, it might be a *date* gaze. Maybe he was thinking something wonderful and romantic, like how her eyes were as gray as the ocean on a cloudy day, when the waves were restless and the sky was—

Bernetta walked directly into a lamppost.

"Bernie Bernie, there's a pole there!" Colin called back to her.

"You all right?" Gabe asked. But Bernetta could tell he was trying not to chuckle.

Bernetta rubbed her forehead with the heel of her hand. "Oh, yeah," she replied. "Just swell."

They reached Sally's Olde Ice Cream Parlour, and Colin studied his flavor choices in the window while Bernetta unzipped her backpack. "Will a twenty work?" she asked Gabe.

"Perfect," he said. He dug a black marker out of his pocket. "I bought this while you guys were at the games. Here, let me see that twenty."

Bernetta handed over the bill, and Gabe wrote on it in careful black letters, just to the right of the White House, *Jordan 555-2986*.

"Great," Bernetta said as Gabe handed the bill back to her. "We all set then?"

Gabe returned the marker to his pocket. "Yep. You and Dracula get some ice cream. I'll be over by the cotton candy"—he checked his watch—"for about fifteen minutes. Remember, you don't know me."

"Sure," Bernetta said. "Good luck."

He looked at her then—gazed, really—right into her stormy sea eyes. "Thanks," he said, and left.

======

Even though it was still morning, there was already a small crowd at the ice-cream shop. Colin danced with his whale while they waited in line.

"Bernie, you like my dancing?" Colin twirled in a circle and lifted the whale high above his head.

Bernetta laughed. "Very nice," she said. "Do you know what flavor you want, Mr. Dracula?"

"Yep yep. Rainbow sherbet and hot fudge."

"Excellent choice."

"I know."

When they got to the front of the line, Bernetta ordered Colin's flavor concoction and a peppermint cone for herself. While the girl behind the counter was scooping, Bernetta put a hand on Colin's shoulder and nodded toward the man at the register. "Hey, Dracula, you want to pay?"

"Aw, how come I got to pay?"

"Because I'm getting the cones, and I don't want you to drop them," Bernetta replied. *Because you're younger and will cause less suspicion.* That was the real reason.

"But *I* wanna—"

"You know, we're probably going to be buying a lot of stuff today, and if you pay every time, I promise that when we get home, I'll give you all my old shoelaces you've been asking for."

Colin's eyes grew huge. "Even the *brown* ones?"

Bernetta nodded. "Even the brown ones." She pulled the twenty from her pocket and handed it to him, phone number side down. "Here, give it to the man like this, okay? With the president showing on the top. They like it better if you do it that way."

"Okay," Colin said, taking the bill. "Hey, Bernie?"

"Yeah?"

"After you give me all your shoelaces, will you help me turn them into ninja weapons?"

"We'll see," she said. "Go pay."

=====

Bernetta and Colin sat on the bench outside the ice-cream parlor, licking their cones. Bernetta was watching the sailboats off in the distance, but Colin was turned around backward, making scary faces at the people passing by. Bernetta's backpack was still strapped securely to her back. She didn't care what

Gabe said about its being *suspicious*. There was over twenty-five hundred dollars in there, and she wasn't taking any chances.

She tucked her feet underneath her Indian-style on the bench and took another lick of ice cream. From the corner of her eye, Bernetta saw Gabe enter the ice-cream store, but she tried not to look at him directly. After all, she reminded herself, she didn't know him at all.

She knew exactly what he was doing, though. Right now he was buying a bottle of water, paying for it with a five-dollar bill. And when the cashier gave him his change, Gabe's face would suddenly switch from smiling to confused. "You gave me change for a five," Gabe would tell the cashier, his cheeks scrunched up as though he didn't quite understand what was going on.

"Yeah?" the cashier would reply. "That's what you gave me."

"No, I didn't," Gabe would say. "It was a twenty. I'm sure of it. I was just looking at it, and there was a phone number written on there. Jordan or something. Look in your drawer if you don't believe me. I'm positive it's there."

Bernetta smiled just thinking about it. It was a

perfect plan, if it worked. And Bernetta was sure it would work. If anyone could pull it off, it was Gabe. He was the best actor of anyone she knew. He could convince anyone of anything.

"Hey, Bernie Bernie," Colin said, tugging on her sleeve.

She wiped the fudge prints off her T-shirt. "What's up, Coliflower?"

"It's your friend." Colin pointed into the souvenir shop across from them.

"My friend?" Bernetta turned around on the bench to look. "You mean Gabe? He's in the ice-cream store."

"No, it's your friend, Bernie. Your best friend." He held his whale up and made it kiss Bernetta's cheek. "You know, Ashley? I saw her over there, looking at the magnets."

Ashley Johansson? Here? Bernetta's stomach did a somersault. It would be just like Ashley to jump back into her life right now, just when things were finally going Bernetta's way again. She narrowed her eyes as she licked a peppermint drip that was making its way down her arm. "Nah, Col," she said. "I don't think that's her." Bernetta could just barely make out a brown-haired girl behind the display of sweatshirts, but there were a billion brown-haired girls in the world. It couldn't be Ashley. Besides, why would she be looking at *refrigerator magnets*?

Colin shrugged and bit a hole in the bottom of his cone. He was sucking the ice cream out when Gabe came over.

"Piece of cake," he said, and he plopped himself down on the bench next to Bernetta.

"They have cake in there?" Colin asked.

"It worked?" Bernetta said.

"Eighteen dollars and fifty cents," Gabe said with a grin. He flashed the money at her. "And half of that is yours."

"Thanks," Bernetta said. She held her hand out for the money, but she was covered in sticky pink ice-cream goo, and it was hard to take off her backpack while holding an ice-cream cone.

Gabe laughed. "Here," he said. "I'll put it in there for you."

"Thanks." Bernetta turned to face Colin while Gabe put the money in her bag. When he'd yanked the zipper up tight, bringing the grand total inside to $2,602.36, Bernetta swiveled back around. "So," she said, "that was pretty easy. You were totally right.

What's the plan now? Try it out at the candy store maybe? Or the T-shirt shack? Or we could take a break and take Colin up the Ferris wheel? He likes when it gets stuck at the top."

Gabe glanced at his watch and then back at Bernetta. "Sorry. What did you say?"

"The Ferris wheel? I thought maybe we could go there next. What do you think?"

"Oh, yeah," Gabe said. "The Ferris wheel. Yeah, that sounds great."

Bernetta raised an eyebrow. "You all right, Gabe?" He seemed to be acting kind of weird all of a sudden. Although what did she know? Elsa said all boys acted weird every once in a while, and you could never know what was going through their heads.

"Yeah, I'm fine," he said. "I just have to go to the bathroom. Why don't I take Colin with me? That kid needs to wash his hands."

"All right," Bernetta said. "Colin, go with Gabe, okay? I'll be right here."

"Grrrr!" Colin replied. He leaped off the bench and grabbed Gabe's hand. "That's Dracula speak for okey-dokey. Watch my whale, 'kay, Bernie? And don't let him bite you."

Gabe turned to go, Colin's hand in his, but then

turned back around. He looked sad about something or—what was the word?—pensive.

"Hey, Bernetta?" he said.

"Yeah?" What was he going to tell her? Was it about her eyes and the stormy sea? She leaned forward on the bench. "Mm-hmm?"

He blinked and looked away quickly. "Nothing," he said. "Never mind." And he and Colin walked off.

Bernetta leaned back on the bench and licked her peppermint ice cream. Boys were infuriating.

They'd been gone only about two minutes, and Bernetta was still licking away at her ice cream and watching the sailboats, when from behind her she heard an angry voice.

"That's her!" someone shouted. "That's the girl right there!"

The voice, Bernetta realized, sounded hideously familiar.

She whirled around, and sure enough, storming toward her, followed by one very large boardwalk security guard, was none other than Ashley Johansson.

Bernetta dropped her ice-cream cone. It landed with a splat right on the wooden boardwalk.

She jumped up as Ashley and the guard came

closer. She had no idea what was going on, but she *did* know that if it involved Ashley Johansson, it couldn't be anything good.

"That's her!" Ashley shouted again. She looked as angry as Bernetta had ever seen her, her nose scrunched up like some crazed bull, ready to charge. "Make her give it back," Ashley told the security guard. She folded her arms across her chest. "She stole it, and it's *mine*."

What? Bernetta's heart was pounding. She wished she knew how to respond, but she didn't even know what was going on. She looked over her shoulder for Gabe and Colin, but they were nowhere in sight.

The guard cleared his throat, and Bernetta took a good look at him. She gulped. He was at least six feet tall, and *big*. He did not have a friendly face either. It was serious, all business. "Let's just take a look, shall we?" He held a beefy hand out to Bernetta. "Would you hand it over, miss?"

Bernetta blinked several times. "Huh? Hand *what* over?"

"The backpack, miss. This girl says it's hers. I'd like to have a look."

"My—no." $2,602.36. That's how much money

was in that backpack. There was no way she was handing that over to Ashley Johansson. But how could Ashley have known the money was in there? Had she seen her with her hands clutched tight around her backpack straps and figured it out? "No!" Bernetta hollered. She wished she could keep her cool, but this was all happening too quickly. It was so fast and terrible. "It's mine," she said. "I've had this back-pack for three years."

Ashley shook her head. "She's lying," she told the guard. "She stole my backpack when I was sitting down on the sand, but she ran away, and I couldn't catch her."

Bernetta stamped her foot, like a two-year-old having a tantrum. "I did *not!*" she cried. "She's making that up. It's mine, I—"

"Please just hand me the bag, miss," the guard said, his hand still outstretched. "Then we can have a look inside and settle this."

Bernetta took a deep breath. "Okay," she said slowly. She sloughed the backpack off her shoulders. She didn't want the guard to question why she had so much cash in there, but at least there was no way Ashley could prove Bernetta had stolen it. And

Bernetta was innocent until proved guilty. Wasn't she?

The guard took the bag and unzipped it, examining the contents. "All right," he said to Ashley. "Can you tell me what's inside here?"

"Well," Ashley said, her voice sharp like a bee sting, "among other things, my *wallet* is in there. That'll prove it's mine."

"What?" Bernetta exclaimed. "There isn't any—"

"Is this it?" the guard asked, producing a slim green wallet.

Bernetta's eyes felt ready to pop right out of her head. Where had that come from? She'd never even seen it before.

"Yeah, that's it," Ashley said. "My school ID is in it."

The guard flipped the wallet open and studied the picture inside. "Ashley Johansson," he read. He took a close look at it. "That's you, all right."

Bernetta felt suddenly dizzy. But she couldn't give up now. There was too much at stake. She wasn't going to lose everything she'd worked for. Not to Ashley Johansson.

"That doesn't prove anything," Bernetta told the guard. "She just put that in there. I don't know how she did it, but she did. It's mine, I swear, and she's the one trying to steal it."

Ashley shook her head. "The backpack's mine," she said. She sounded calm now, confident. "My name's on it," she told the guard. "Underneath the flap, by the zipper. Right at the top."

Bernetta snorted. "No, it's not. What are you—"

She never finished her sentence. Because the guard lifted up the zipper flap, and there, as plain as anything, was a name in large capital letters:

ASHLEY JOHANSSON

15

[
illusion *n:* a magical effect that appears impossible but that is in fact accomplished through real-world means; often refers to larger stage tricks
]

A s they rode home on the bus, Bernetta and Gabe seated just behind Colin and his whale, Bernetta did her best to hold back her tears. She'd never been so miserable. Not when she'd been framed for the cheating ring, not even when she'd lost her scholarship. How did Ashley always manage to beat her? Bernetta never even stood a chance. She wiped at her eyes with the back of her hand. She might as well cry, she decided. There was nothing else to do now. Her life was over.

"Are you okay, Bernetta?" Gabe asked.

"No," she said. The word came out as three separate syllables.

Gabe bit his bottom lip. "Oh. Sorry."

Was she *okay*? How could she possibly be *okay*? Bernetta was pretty sure she'd never be okay again. Not only had she lost $2,602.36, the money she'd worked an entire month to get, but sooner or later her mother was going to figure out that she hadn't deposited a single dime in her checking account. And when she figured that out, there were going to be questions. Lots and lots of questions. With a third of her summer already gone, Bernetta was suddenly penniless, and Ashley Johansson was richer than ever. She'd never go back to Mount Olive, and her parents would figure out the truth.

"So what happened, anyway?" Gabe said, picking at the edge of a Superman sticker that was stuck to the back of Colin's seat. "I mean, I know she took your backpack, but how did she—"

"I don't know *how* she did it," Bernetta said with a sniff. "There's no way she could've—but her *name* was on it. I just—I don't know what I'm going to do."

Gabe ripped off a corner of the sticker. "I'm sorry," he said, but softer this time. "That's awful. I can't believe she did that."

"That's because you don't know her," Bernetta said, wrapping her arms around her stomach. She kept her voice low, so Colin wouldn't hear her. "I should've seen it coming."

"But you couldn't have known—"

"I should've known she'd try *something*! Of course she would. She's *Ashley*. I should have known she'd try to mess with me again."

"I'm sorry."

"And she thinks I'm just some idiot, this huge moron she can stomp all over. And you know what? I *am*. I am a moron."

"You're not a moron."

"Of course I am. She's used me twice, and I didn't see it coming at all! I just let her do it. I even used to think she was my friend. Can you believe that? I actually *trusted* her."

"Look, Bernetta," Gabe said, "it's not your fault. You're a good person, you know? And she's not. And no matter how much money she has, you'll always be better than her."

Bernetta watched the houses speeding by outside. "But it's not just the money. She was so *nice* when I first met her. She was my best friend. She really was. We'd do everything together. And then, one day, she just switched, like, like—"

"Like Gollum," Gabe said, nodding seriously.

"Gollum?" Bernetta asked.

"Yeah. You know. From *The Lord of the Rings*? Frodo thinks he can trust him, that he's going to lead him and Sam straight to Mordor, and then the next thing he knows, he's in the middle of Shelob's lair. Remember? That giant spider who tries to eat him?"

Bernetta couldn't help laughing, although she'd been crying so hard, half of it came out as a cough. "Okay," she said, "you're right. She's Gollum."

"See? And at the end Gollum falls into Mount Doom and Frodo and Sam make it home okay. So you'll be fine too. I promise."

Bernetta sighed. "I guess."

"Look," Gabe said, "I know you lost all that money, but don't worry, okay? We still have almost two whole months. We can do it."

"Nine thousand dollars," Bernetta said. The number sounded bigger than it ever had before. "I need nine *thousand* dollars, Gabe. And I don't have anything."

"I know it's a lot, but there are all sorts of—"

"What's the point?" Bernetta said. "I mean, really. What if Ashley just takes it again? What's the point of even trying?"

Gabe opened his mouth like he was going to say something but then closed it again. They were silent until the bus stopped at Fields Street.

"That's my house right there," Gabe said, pointing out the window as he stood up. "Come by on Monday, all right? I'll figure something out."

Bernetta shrugged. "I'll think about it."

When the bus started moving again, Colin plopped down into the seat next to her. "Hey, Bernie Bernie, why are you crying? You want my whale to tell you a joke and cheer you up? He's really good at knock-knock ones. Except you have to do the ending part yourself, because sometimes he forgets how it goes."

———

Bernetta and Colin got home long before their mother, and Bernetta spent most of that time panicking. First she called the bank to find out when she could expect her bank statement. They told her not to worry, that it should be there in a little less than a month.

"And don't forget," the woman on the phone told her, "you can always check your balance online anytime you want."

"Wonderful," Bernetta said. "Thanks so much."

Then she worried about what to tell her mom about babysitting. "Mom"—she practiced in front of the mirror—"Hank got sick at the last minute, so Mrs. Norton told me not to babysit. He had a fever and everything. So I took Colin to the pier. He had a great time. We got ice cream, and he won a whale."

That sounded convincing, right?

She went downstairs and found Colin sitting on the living-room floor, tying her old shoelaces into giant knots. "Hey, um, Colin?" she said.

He put his hands on his head and looked up at her. "Geeble gabble?"

"Yeah . . ." She took in a deep breath. "So, you know . . . today at the pier . . . you had fun, right?"

Colin nodded. "Yep. You wanna see my ninja shoelaces? This is how they work. You hold on right here, and then you swing it at the bad guys and—"

"Colin, come on, I'm trying to tell you something important."

He closed his eyes and began to spin the shoelaces in wild circles around his head.

"Colin, I really have to—"

"*Ninja attack!*" he shouted.

"Colin!"

The front door opened. "Hey, you two!" their mother called. "You're home already!" She set her keys on the table by the door. "How did everything go today?"

Before Bernetta could even remember the first line

of the lie she'd practiced in the mirror, Colin lunged into their mother's arms. "Hank's sick!" he shouted. "He's cool, but he's really, really big for a six-year-old. And Mom? We had a really good time. I wanna go with Bernie again next week."

"Oh," their mother replied, "well, that's wonderful. Bernetta, can you help me unload the groceries from the car?"

"Um . . ." Bernetta looked at Colin, and he smiled back at her. "Sure."

Well, that was one less thing to worry about, at least.

––––––

Sunday evening Bernetta lay backward on her bed, her feet up on the wall and her grip tight around an old copy of *Ender's Game*. But she wasn't really reading. She was chewing and thinking.

All weekend long Bernetta had tried to come up with a way to solve her problems, but it was impossible. There was no way to fix things. She couldn't make nine thousand dollars in two months. Even if she could, her mother was bound to check her bank balance soon and realize something was wrong. Really, there was no other option but to turn herself in and get it over with. Bernetta was going to go downstairs and tell her parents exactly what she had been up to. As soon as she finished chapter seven.

Bernetta hadn't turned a page in twenty minutes.

It just didn't make sense, Bernetta thought. *How* had Ashley pulled it off? The way that name had just appeared on her backpack like that, like magic. How on earth could she have—

Wait a minute.

Magic? Bernetta turned around and sat up straight in her bed, tucking her legs underneath her. She chewed on her book page a little harder, gears turning in her head.

If there was one thing Bernetta Wallflower, magician's assistant, knew for a fact, it was that there was no such thing as magic. Illusions, sure. But real magic simply didn't exist. Maybe it *looked* like magic when you ripped a jack of diamonds out of a sourdough bread roll, but the trick lost some of its sparkle once you knew that a gray-haired waiter had placed a special basket of bread with a card already inside it right in front of you. The card didn't *appear*. It had been planted there all along.

Bernetta stopped chewing. She took in a deep breath of air, then let it out very slowly.

Suddenly she got the feeling that she'd spent the past four weeks staring at Gabe's right hand, when all along he'd been hiding a quarter in his left.

16

> **revelation** *n:* the act of discovering an object or a piece of information previously unknown; often the finale of a trick

It was a good thing Gabe's house was only one story high. That meant Bernetta didn't have to climb any trees in order to pound on his bedroom window first thing Monday morning.

She peered through a gap in the curtain to make sure it was Gabe's room. His bed was right next to the window, and she could see him sleeping peacefully. "Hey!" Bernetta hollered, banging on the glass with her fist. "Hey! Wake up!"

Gabe sat up in bed with a start and looked toward the window, rubbing at his eyes. "Huh? What's going—"

"Wake up!" Bernetta pounded on the glass again.

Gabe looked nervous, but when he pulled back the curtain and saw Bernetta, his face relaxed. "Oh," he said, "it's you." He threw back his covers and sat up in bed to open the window. "You kind of freaked me out, Bernetta," he said with a smile. "What time is it anyway?"

Bernetta glared at him, plaid pajamas and all. Yesterday she might have thought his hair looked sort of cute, all tousled like that, but now she was wiser and completely unfazed by messy-cute boy hair.

She set her palms down flat on the windowsill and leaned in, putting her weight as far forward as possible. She was pretty sure this made her look intimidating. She was going to roast him now. *Mess with Bernetta Wallflower,* she thought, *and you're as good as dead.*

Too bad she didn't *feel* intimidating.

"Bernetta?" Gabe asked. "Something wrong?"

Bernetta sighed a deep sigh and scratched a bug bite on her arm. She couldn't roast him. She just couldn't. She looked at him then, dead in the eye, and she could feel her entire face crumple. Her voice came out tiny and thin.

"Why did you do it?" she asked. "Why did you write her name on my backpack?"

He didn't deny it. And he didn't call Bernetta an

idiot either. His face crumpled too, just like a napkin. "I'm so sorry," he said. And then he sat back on his bed and stared at his hands. "I'm sorry," he said again.

Bernetta bit her bottom lip. Her eyes were brimming with tears, and she wasn't even sure why. She'd been betrayed before. *That* was nothing new. And it wasn't like she and Gabe were best friends or anything. She'd known him only a month. Still, it hurt. Right in the center of her stomach. It hurt something awful.

"So it's true?" Bernetta asked. Her voice was almost a whisper. "You set me up? I mean, all along, you were— You never even—"

Gabe nodded. "I'm sorry." It seemed to be all he could say.

"But why? Why would you do that? You didn't even know me."

Gabe looked up at her then, with the saddest eyes Bernetta had ever seen. "I was friends with her," he said. "Ashley. Back when she still went to Kingsfield with me." He shook his head. "We did all kinds of stupid stuff. Shoplifting, stealing kids' lunch money from their backpacks, even the kindergartners. We set up this whole gambling thing too, and we'd rake in money from the middle school soccer games. It was crazy. We thought we were fifth-grade bookies or something. I don't know. It was exciting, I guess. You never knew what was going to happen with Ashley around."

You never knew, all right, Bernetta thought. All of a sudden the sight of Gabe in his pajamas was making her sick. How could she ever have *liked* him? When all this time he was *using* her? She was just a part of one of his cons. What was it called, the mark? The victim. Bernetta was the mark for a perfectly choreographed long con, starring Ashley Johansson as the expert con artist. And Gabe had been the roper.

"But," Gabe continued, "then I found out she was going to a new school, Mount Olive, and I was kind of relieved. Because well, things were getting out of hand. I had to, I don't know, watch my back all the time. I guess I was just getting tired."

"So?" Bernetta said, drumming her fingers on the windowsill. "Why didn't you just quit? If she left your school, why didn't you just cut things off with her?"

"I did!" Gabe said. "I tried to. But . . ." He heaved another deep sigh, as though just the memory of what he was about to say made the air around him harder to breathe. "Right before Ashley found out her parents were sending her to a new school, we made this bet. Me and Ashley. It was her idea, and it was totally crazy. I never really thought she was *serious* about it."

Bernetta tucked a strand of hair behind her ear. She wished she could just walk away right then and there. Gabe didn't deserve to have anyone listen to his stupid stories. But she was curious despite herself. "What was the bet?" she asked.

"Well, Ashley was always bragging about how great she was at making money. She said she could make five thousand dollars in one year, just pulling stuff on kids at school, and she'd never even get caught. Back then I thought it was ridiculous. Five thousand dollars? I mean, we did pretty good, but we only made a couple hundred bucks the whole year of fifth grade. And I thought we were millionaires, you know? But Ashley was always talking about five thousand dollars. That was her big number. So somehow I got roped into this bet with her. She said if she couldn't make five thousand dollars in one year, then she'd have to give me half of what she *had* made. And if she did make the money—" He stopped talking then and chewed on a fingernail.

Bernetta leaned a fraction of an inch closer into the

window. "If she did make the money . . ." she prompted.

Gabe spat out a bit of nail. "Then I'd have to match her," he finished.

"What do you mean, match her?" Bernetta asked.

"You know, I'd owe her as much money as she made."

Bernetta raised her eyebrows. "Five thousand dollars? You'd owe her five thousand dollars?" He nodded. "But that's crazy! Why would you ever agree to that?"

"I thought it was impossible! I didn't think there was any way she could do it. I thought I'd be making easy money."

"You should've known better."

Gabe groaned. "You're telling me." He went back to chewing on his thumbnail. "Ever seen *Guys and Dolls*? There's this one line, where Marlon Brando is talking about betting, and he says that if someone ever tries to bet on something ridiculous, like that they can make a jack of spades jump out of a deck of cards and squirt cider in your ear, you shouldn't take it, because no matter what, you're going to end up with an earful of cider."

Bernetta couldn't help smiling. Only Gabe could think about *movies* at a time like this. But then she frowned again. Gabe wasn't the only one with cider in his ear. She'd fallen for his bets too, hadn't she? With the grandmother and the bookstore gift card and the movie quotes. Gabe wasn't exactly a poor, pitiful victim in all this. Bernetta couldn't believe she'd ever thought he had *chocolate* eyes. They were mud. Mud, plain and simple. She turned around and slid down until she was sitting on the grass, back leaning against the house. She folded her arms across her chest.

"So then what?" she said up toward Gabe. "So Ashley made the five thousand, and you owed her big, and then what happened? How did I get involved?"

"Well, yeah," he said. Bernetta could just barely see that he'd leaned his head out the window to talk to her, but she didn't look at him. "She went to Mount Olive for sixth grade and made all that money. I couldn't believe she did it, but she showed me the cash herself. And she told me how she did it, with that cheating ring, slipping those notes in everyone's lockers. And she told me about you, too, and how she could never get caught because she'd pinned it all on you, used you as a—as a scapegoat or whatever."

Bernetta could feel her insides tightening up. "Did she tell you I thought she was my best friend?" she said. She wiped the tears away quick. There was no way she going to let Gabe know she was *crying*. "Did she tell you that she used to spend the night at my house and bake cookies with me and my little brother? And that she let me tell her all my secrets and pretended like she *cared*?" In all that time, Bernetta realized, she hadn't known Ashley at all. Because in all that time Ashley had never said one word about Gabe.

"No," Gabe said, and he began to speak more slowly. "I didn't know any of that." He paused. "I didn't. . . . See, all of a sudden I owed her a ton of money, and I didn't know what to do. I knew that if I didn't give it to her, I'd . . . well, I knew it would be bad. She said I had until the end of the summer. She said I should've been saving up all along, that I should've known I was going to have to pay her. But I didn't think I could do it. And I figured if she'd made all this money by setting you up . . ." He paused again. "Well, I thought I could too."

"You thought I sounded gullible, right?" she said. "You thought I'd make a good mark."

"But I didn't even know you then!" Gabe said. "And now that I do, I'm sorry I ever—"

"So is that why you went to my dad's club that

night? So you could rope me into something?"

He sighed. "Yeah," he said. "I don't even know what I was thinking. I was desperate. Ashley told me you worked there on Saturdays, so I convinced Patrick to have his birthday party there. I didn't find out until later that you'd just gotten in trouble for Ashley's whole thing at school."

Bernetta wiped her wet hands on her shorts. "I think I should go," she said into the air.

"No!" Gabe cried. "Wait. Please." And before Bernetta knew what was happening, Gabe had crawled out his window and was sitting right beside her on the grass in his blue plaid pajamas. "Look," he said, and he put a hand on Bernetta's knee. She sucked in a quick gasp of air but turned her head the other way. He kept talking. "Bernetta, I went there, and I met you, and you did that watch trick, you know? And I realized right then that I couldn't do it. You weren't like Ashley, you weren't like anyone I knew at all, and I don't know, I guess I . . . liked you."

Bernetta didn't know if Gabe meant he liked her or he *liked* her, but she refused to look at him either way.

"I knew I couldn't do it," Gabe said. "You didn't deserve that. So I decided I'd just leave you alone and find some other way to make the money, but then I ran into you again, and I swear I thought it was *fate*, just like in *Close Encounters*, how I said, with the potatoes. And I needed money, and you needed money, so I thought we should be partners. And we were really good partners. I was right. Bonnie and Clyde."

Bernetta wiped the last of her tears away and looked down at her knee. Gabe's hand was still there. She looked him in the eyes again and then shook her head, drawing her legs in close and wrapping her arms around them. Gabe took his hand back. He seemed hurt about it. Good.

"That's a nice story and everything," Bernetta said, sniffling her very last sniffle, "but I know you're still lying."

"I'm not!" Gabe cried. "I swear!"

"Oh, yeah?" Bernetta was done being upset now. She was *mad*. "Well, if that's true, if you thought we made such great partners, if you *liked* me or whatever, then explain why you set me up. Tell me exactly why you put Ashley's wallet in my backpack, Gabe, and why you wrote her name on there so she could steal everything right out from under me. Hmm? Why'd you do it?"

Gabe closed his eyes and leaned all the way back,

resting his head against the side of the house. He pressed his knuckles against his eyes and was quiet for a long while. He seemed to be thinking, but Bernetta couldn't tell if he was angry at himself or busy coming up with new lies.

"I just . . ." he said at last, opening his eyes and staring straight ahead as he spoke. "I guess when I saw all that money you had that day, I just went a little crazy or something. And I thought that if I could get it from you, then I could give it to Ashley along with what I'd made too, and I'd be done. I'd never have to worry about her anymore. So I called her, and I—I told her about the money in your backpack. And she came up with that idea, that I should put her wallet in there and everything. She thought it up, I swear."

"But you did it."

Gabe scratched at the side of his face. "Yeah. Yeah, I did."

They were quiet for a long time again, both of them staring straight ahead in silence. Bernetta noticed that they were breathing right in time with each other, in and out, and she tried to change the rhythm of her breaths so they wouldn't match Gabe's anymore, but it was a hard thing to do once you started to think about it.

"Bernetta? I'm just—I need to say I'm sorry. I mean, I know I said it before, but it's true. I'm really sorry. I never should have done it, and I wish I hadn't. I've been thinking about it since Friday, and I—I need to make it up to you. I want to get your money back, Bernetta. I want to help you. And I think I know how we can do it."

"Gabe ..." Bernetta said softly, but he cut her off.

"It's a long con. You know, how I was telling you before, like in *The Sting*? I found one we can actually do. Wait, I'll show you."

He leaped up, leaned in through his open window, and stood on his toes as he tried to reach something. When he slid back down to the ground, he was holding a book, a thick one entitled *Hoaxes and Scams: A Compendium of Deceptions, Ruses, and Swindles*. He began to flip through the pages frantically.

"I was looking at this before I went to sleep last night. I thought we might find something in here we could use to get your money back. And look. Look right here." He smoothed his hands across a page. "'Green goods swindle,'" he read. "'Counterfeit money con game.' Bernetta, it's perfect. We can totally do this."

Bernetta hoisted herself off the ground and wiped off her shorts. "I'm gonna go now," she said softly.

"But"—Gabe got to his feet too—"you can't just leave, Bernetta. Look, I know we can pull this off. It's perfect for us. And we can get your Mount Olive money back. I'll give you all the profits. Everything. One hundred percent. I owe you. Please."

Bernetta took one last look in his eyes, and yes, she was certain they were chocolate after all. But chocolate could be bad for you too. She looked down at her feet and dug the toe of her sneaker into the lawn.

"How do I know I can trust you anymore?" she said.

Gabe shook his head slowly. "I guess you can't," he answered with a frown. "I mean, you shouldn't. Not really. Not anymore. But . . ." He looked up, and Bernetta thought he might almost be grinning. "Well . . . *do* you?"

Bernetta bit her lip and thought about that. It was a very good question.

<hr>

Even though Bernetta knew it was probably the stupidest thing she would ever do in her entire life, she agreed to trust Gabe. Just one last time. One last con. They spent the morning planning and scheming, poring over details on the floor of Gabe's room. They tried to work through every moment, and plan for every scenario, so that no matter what happened, they'd always be in control of the game. There were phone calls to make, numbers to crunch, and stratagems to plan. And late that afternoon, when they couldn't think of any more wrinkles to straighten out, Gabe made Bernetta watch *The Sting* with him. They sat side by side on Gabe's living-room couch, a bowl of popcorn between them. There was no more knee touching, but Bernetta was okay with that for the time being.

When Gabe paused the movie to get up for more soda, Bernetta plucked a loose thread from the couch. "So where are your parents, anyway?" she called into the kitchen.

Gabe appeared in the doorway with two cans of root beer. "At work. Why?"

"Don't they care that you're alone all day?"

Gabe shrugged. "Most summers I go to camp, but my dad missed the application deadline this year, so my parents decided I'd be fine by myself. Anyway, it's not like I'm bored or anything." He tossed her a soda. "I've been hanging out with you."

Bernetta looked around the room as she took a sip of root beer. Besides the giant bookshelf crammed with more movies than Bernetta had ever seen, the house looked pretty normal. "I thought you were rich," Bernetta said. "You said you were raised by a nanny."

Gabe plopped down next to her on the couch and reached for the remote control. "I lied," he said, but he was grinning.

"Oh," Bernetta replied. "Well"—she grabbed a couch pillow behind her—"just don't do it again, all right?" And she tossed the pillow at his head.

"Deal," he said. And he lobbed it right back.

17

> ☞ **forced card** *n:* a card that the spectator
> believes he has chosen of his own free will
> but that has been unknowingly forced upon
> him by the magician

The next morning Bernetta had trouble keeping her eyes open as she chomped on her toast. It had been a long night, with numbers and schemes and plans whizzing through her head, and she'd hardly slept a wink, worrying about the big con she and Gabe were planning.

Across the breakfast table her dad took a bite of oatmeal as she got up to put her plate in the sink. "Hey, Bernie?" he said.

She turned. "Yeah, Dad?"

"I know you've been busy lately, but I was wondering if you'd had any time to work on the French Drop at all."

"Oh." She ran some water over her plate. "Um,

yeah," she lied. "Yeah, I'm getting pretty good."

"Well, I'd love to see it when you think you have it down."

"Sure." As she passed the table, she gave him a quick peck on the cheek. "Sure thing, Dad."

"Oh, and I think it's wonderful you're taking Colin to the Nortons' with you again, Bernie. He really seems to like Hank."

Bernetta smiled. "Yeah, I think he does."

Colin dashed into the room at that moment. "BernieBernieBernie, wait for meeeeeee!"

"I'm waiting, I'm waiting," she said with a laugh. "You ready, Colombo?"

"Yeah. I got my rain boots on, see?" Colin lifted up his feet in turn, showing off his bright yellow galoshes with bug eyeballs on the toes.

"Colin, it's not raining."

"Yeah, but this way, if the giant slugs come, I won't have to step in any of their slime."

Bernetta's father got up from the table and knocked on the top of Colin's head. "Good thinking, kiddo. Have fun, you two."

"We will, Dad," Bernetta said as she took Colin's hand and headed out the door.

They met Gabe on the corner of Warner and Burnett. He gave Colin a high five. "Nice boots," he told him.

"They're for the slugs," Colin replied.

Gabe nodded seriously. "I would've worn mine, but they had holes in them."

"You can borrow one of mine if you want," Colin told him.

"I might have to."

The plan for today, the first part of their long con, was to storm over to Ashley's house and demand Bernetta's money back. They were going as a force, a unit. Hopefully, she'd never see it coming, never know what hit her.

Beside her, Colin was busy stomping in imaginary puddles or squishing invisible slugs, or something.

"Hey, Colin!" Bernetta said. "You want to play a game?"

"Yep." He ran forward three steps, took a giant leap, then stopped walking. "I mean, maybe," he called back to her. "What is it?"

"It's called"—Bernetta looked over at Gabe—"I say, you say."

"How's it work?" Colin asked.

"Well, I say something, then you repeat it, and then you say it as many times as you can. Over and over and over and—"

"And over and over and over and over . . ."

Bernetta laughed. "Good. But you can only say the special words me and Gabe tell you, 'kay?"

"Okay, I'm ready, Bernie Bernie. Gimme a really good one."

"All right. Um, pineapple."

"Pineapple!" Colin cried. "Pineapple pineapple pineapple . . ."

Gabe leaned in close to Bernetta as they continued walking. "He catches on quick."

Bernetta nodded. "Yep. You give him one."

"Hippopotamus!" Gabe called out.

"Hippopotamus! Hippopotamus hippopotamus hippopotamus hippopotamus hippopotamus . . ."

———

By the time they got to Ashley's, Colin was a pro at I say, you say, and Bernetta and Gabe were running out of words to give him. "We're here!" Bernetta called out.

"Topeka, Kansas!" Colin replied, still engrossed in the game. "Topeka, Kansas! Topeka, Kans—"

"Just ring the doorbell, 'kay?"

Colin rang Ashley's doorbell with his thumb. Ashley's mother answered.

"Bernetta!" she squealed, and wrapped her arms

around her in a hug. She smelled like coffee and fresh-baked waffles. "It's been so long. What have you been up to this summer? We've missed you."

Well, Mrs. Johansson, after your daughter framed me and I lost my scholarship for next year, I took up thievery, but then she stole that money off me too, so now I'm about to pull a long con. Sorry I haven't really had the time to stop by.

"I've, um, been at camp," she said at last. "Is Ashley home?"

"Sure." She smiled. "And Gabe!" she cried out. "Why, I hardly recognized you. You must have grown a foot! It's certainly been a while since you stopped by to visit."

Gabe kicked his feet against the welcome mat. "Yeah, um, sorry about that."

"Oh, don't worry, sweetie. It's good to see you. Why don't you all come in? I'll get Ashley. I think she's still asleep." She led them inside. "Have a seat right there on the couch. Ashley dear! You have visitors!" And she scurried down the hallway.

Gabe cleared his throat as they all settled themselves on the fluffy beige couch. "This is probably going to be weird," he whispered to Bernetta.

"You're telling me," she said.

"Hippopotamus hippopotamus hippopotamus," Colin said. "Hippopotamus."

Mrs. Johansson came back into the room then, with Ashley padding right behind her. She was still wearing her pajamas, which consisted of a pink tank top with the words DON'T BUG ME WHEN I'M SNOOZING written on the front, and a pair of flannel shorts covered in ballerina bunnies. Her hair was piled on top of her head in a messy ponytail. Her face fell when she saw them.

"Here you go, Ash," her mother said. "Your friends dropped by for a visit, isn't that sweet? Ashley, have a seat. Be a good hostess now. Anybody want some orange juice? Freshly squeezed. I'll just go get some."

Ashley perched herself on the edge of the armchair, and for several minutes the only person who said anything at all was Colin, still reciting silly words from the walk over. But once Mrs. Johansson had left them to "chat and catch up," after handing them each a tall glass of orange juice—that's when things got ugly.

Ashley's eyes darted from Bernetta to Gabe and back again. "What are you two morons doing here?" she asked.

"I want my money back," Bernetta replied. Her hand was shaking as she gripped her glass. She did her best to steady it. "You stole it, and it's mine, so you have to give it back."

"Right," Ashley said. "Like that's going to happen."

"I need it back," Bernetta said, trying to sound forceful. "All of it. Today."

"Just give it to her, Ashley," Gabe said.

"Toenails!" Colin shouted. "Toenails toenails toenails toenails!"

Ashley ignored him and turned to Gabe. "So, dimwad," she said, "you tell your new girlfriend how you set her up?" She smiled at Bernetta. "Bet you didn't know about that, did you, Bernetta? I bet you thought he actually *liked* you?"

Bernetta folded her arms over her chest. "How much you want to bet, Ashley? Five thousand dollars?"

"Tomato juice and cucumbers!" Colin chanted. "Tomato juice and cucumbers."

Gabe shook his head. "She already knows, Ashley. I told her."

"Tomato juice and cucumbers."

Ashley calmly examined her fingernails. They were pale pink, no chips in the polish. "I'm not giving the money back," she said. "It's mine. Gabe owed it to me. Why don't you take it up with him?"

"Tomato juice and cucumbers!"

"Can't the stupid kid say anything else?" Ashley hollered.

"I'm just playing I say, you say," Colin said. "Bernetta and Hank taught it to me."

Gabe grinned at him. "And you're really good at it too, buddy. But why don't you try one of the other words we told you?" He gave Colin a thumbs-up.

"Okay," Colin said, drumming his fingers on the edge of the couch. He seemed to be thinking hard. "Um . . ."

Ashley rolled her eyes. "*Anyway*," she said, "this has been fun and everything, but you might as well go home. There's no way I'm ever going to—"

Colin bolted upright in his seat. "Counterfixed money!" he screeched.

Bernetta sucked in a quick breath of air, and next to her, Gabe started coughing.

Ashley suddenly looked interested. "What did you say?" she asked Colin.

"Counterfixed money, counterfixed money, counterfixed money . . ."

"Colin," Bernetta whispered. "Colorado River— that's enough."

"Counterfixed money, counterfixed money . . ."

"Colin!"

Colin turned to her, eyes wide. "What, Bernie Bernie? I'm just playing the game like you said. I'm repeating the funny words you and Hank told me."

Gabe coughed again. "We never said that word, Col." He turned to Ashley. "He made that one up."

"Nuh-uh," Colin said. "You guys said 'counterfixed money' about one million times today. I heard you." Gabe squeezed his eyes shut tight. "Anyway," Colin continued, "I don't even know what that means. Ashley, what does 'counterfixed' mean?"

Bernetta pulled her brother onto her lap and smiled at Ashley. "Don't listen to him," she said. "He doesn't know what he's talking about."

Ashley looked from Colin to Gabe and at last settled her gaze on Bernetta. "Maybe not," she said. "But I think *I* do. And I definitely want in."

———

No matter how Bernetta and Gabe haggled, Ashley would not change her mind. She informed them pretty clearly that if they didn't let her in on the counterfeiting deal, she'd find a way to make both their lives utterly miserable. Worse, she'd foul up their plans. No Mount Olive money for Bernetta. Maybe even jail. They left her house with a new partner in their counterfeiting scam and absolutely zero money.

They headed to the park. Bernetta couldn't take Colin home until after she was done "babysitting," so he spent hours chasing other kids around the jungle gym with his hands in his rain boots like yellow "bug monsters," hanging upside down from the monkey bars, and burying things in the sandbox. Gabe and Bernetta passed most of the time playing tetherball. Gabe kept trying to talk to her about some movie with a giant monster housefly in it, but Bernetta wasn't paying much attention. Her head was spinning with all the things that could possibly go wrong tomorrow with Ashley. It seemed like a whole lot of things.

"Bernie Bernie!" Colin called over to her. "Come here, 'kay? I wanna bury you in *sand*! Hank too!"

Bernetta and Gabe headed over to join Colin in the sandbox, and Colin instructed them to remove their shoes. "I'm gonna cover your whole feet in quick-sand," he told them. "Then you'll be trapped forever until it's time to go home."

As Bernetta peeled off her socks, she caught sight of her Blueberry Bramble toenails, and she quickly stuck them deep in the sand. What would Elsa think of all this? Bernetta wondered. What would her sister say if she knew about Bernetta's new life as a con artist?

Same Old Netta was changing, all right. But Bernetta couldn't help worrying that maybe she was changing a little too much.

Gabe looked over at her as Colin began to pour buckets of sand over their legs. "You know, Bernetta," Gabe told her, "it'll go fine tomorrow. I promise. Everything will be just fine."

Would it?

When Bernetta got home, she dug the polish remover out of Elsa's dresser drawer, and one by one, she erased the last of the blue paint from her toenails.

18

> ☞ **three-card monte** *n:* a game in which
> the spectator must attempt to follow the
> movement of one specific card among three

The next morning Bernetta was supposed to meet Gabe and go pick up Ashley at her house so they all could head off together to start their counterfeit money scheme. But when she opened her front door to step outside, there was already one major calamity waiting for her on the lawn. Ashley Johansson was standing right beside the mailbox, with one hand on the handlebar of her bike and the other one on her hip, a black canvas purse dangling from her arm. Her bike tires were flattening the Wallflowers' grass in two ugly lines.

"Ashley!" Bernetta hissed, closing the door quickly behind her. "What are you doing here? What if my parents see you? They think I'm babysitting! We were supposed to meet at *your* house!"

"Right." Ashley snorted. "Like I'm falling for that one."

Bernetta let out a huff. "Fine. Let's just get going, all right?"

Ashley was going to be a handful, that was for sure.

———

Gabe stood beside his bike, waiting, at the corner of Zottola and Ziegler. His orange T-shirt read COFFEE, TEA, OR DEATH? He raised his eyebrows when he saw them approaching. "Change of plans?" he asked Bernetta.

Bernetta jerked her head in Ashley's direction. "She thought we were going to ditch her," she said.

"Aw, Ashley, we wouldn't do *that*," Gabe said. "We like you too much. You're always so nice to everyone."

"Hey, dimwad, can we just get going already?"

"See?" Gabe said, with a wink to Bernetta. "Nice and polite." He slung his leg over his bike and sat down on the seat. "Follow me," he told them, and they pedaled into town. They passed the supermarket Bernetta's parents shopped at, passed the movie theater, passed several restaurants. When they finally reached the strip mall, Gabe stopped pedaling.

"There," he said, planting his feet firmly on the ground. "That's it."

Ashley screeched her bike to a stop. "What's it?" she said.

"Right there," Gabe told her, pointing.

"The shoe store? We're going to buy counterfeit money at a *shoe* store?"

"Um, could you maybe not be so loud about it?" Bernetta said, wiping the sweat off the back of her neck.

Gabe just shrugged. "This is where the guy told us to come on the phone," he said.

Ashley shook her head like she couldn't believe what kinds of idiots she was working with, but she parked her bike beside the door to the shoe store. "Well?" she said. "You guys coming or aren't you?"

Bernetta swung her leg over her bike. "Jeez," she whispered to Gabe, "you'd think this whole thing was her idea."

As they walked into the store, a bell on the door let out a loud clang. Bernetta couldn't help noticing the BLOWOUT SALE signs everywhere and how empty the shelves were. The store was empty too, actually. Besides the man behind the counter and the woman packing shoes into boxes in the corner, there was no one inside.

Gabe let out a low whistle and turned to the man. "Business hasn't been so good lately, huh?" he said.

The man coughed, as though noticing his customers for the first time, and lowered his chin, glaring down his nose at Gabe. He had a trim little mustache, and his gray hair was slicked back. "You kids need help with something?"

Bernetta fingered a belt loop on her khaki shorts. "Um, we're here to see Mike?"

"There's no one named Mike here," the man said. "I think you kids got the wrong shoe store."

Bernetta stood up straight, trying to look older, more serious. "We made some calls yesterday," she said. "We talked to Bruce. He said to come here."

The man scratched his mustache with three fingers. "Bruce, huh?" His gaze darted from Bernetta to Gabe to Ashley. "You here for the special shoes?"

Gabe nodded. "Yeah," he said. "The special shoes."

The man clicked his tongue. "Well, I keep them in the back," he said. "Right this way. Val?" he called to the woman in the corner. "Can you keep an eye on things out here?"

He opened a door to the storeroom and motioned them inside. The air was thick with the scent of leather and new rubber, and the narrow shelves were stacked high with boxes and boxes of shoes. It was a tight squeeze, but somehow they all fitted inside. The man shut the door behind them.

He crossed his arms and stared at them for a moment, licking his bottom lip. "Shouldn't you kids be in school or something?" he said at last.

There was barely room for Gabe to shake his head. "It's *summer*," he replied.

"Well, you shouldn't be here," the man told them. "I never worked with kids before. I don't like it. How old are all of you, anyway?"

For the first time Ashley spoke. "None of your business," she said. "You know why we're here. That's all that matters."

The man turned his mouth into the smallest of smiles. "So you're the leader of the bunch, huh?" he said to Ashley. "Fine then. But you didn't get this counterfeit dough from me, all right? For all you kids know, my name really is Mike, we clear?"

Gabe nodded. "Nice to meet you, Mike," he said. "I'm Alan Smithee. This right here"—he pointed to

Bernetta—"is Carlotta Gauss, and that's Carlotta's cousin, Lizzie. Lizzie Borden."

"How's this work exactly?" Ashley asked Mike.

"Well, Lizzie," he said, "it works like this. You give me cash, and I give you the counterfeit dough. Each fake twenty costs five dollars. Pretty simple. Some people like to try out a sample first, so if you want, you lay down fifty and I'll give you a small amount of the stuff. You try it out on the local vendors, see how it goes over, and then you come back and tell me how much you want. I guarantee, it's next to perfect. Even a banker would swear up and down it was real. If you like it, you come back and give me a deposit for your order. Half the money in cash today, and I'll bring you the goods tomorrow."

Ashley squinted. "I don't like the sound of that last bit, about the deposit."

"We *told* you yesterday," Bernetta said, but Gabe coughed in her direction, and she stopped talking.

"I still don't like it," Ashley said.

"I don't care if you don't like it," Mike told her, squaring his shoulders. "I've been doing business since you were in diapers, and that's the way it works."

Ashley glared at him. "Okay, *fine*," she said. "We'll try it out." She turned to Bernetta. "*Carlotta,* why don't you give Mike here fifty bucks?"

"Actually, *Lizzie*," Bernetta said, "I don't have fifty bucks. Someone decided to steal my—"

Gabe jabbed an elbow into her side. "I have fifty," he told Mike, digging into his pocket. "Lizzie, you can pay me back later."

"Sure thing," Ashley replied with a sugar-sweet smile. Bernetta wondered about that smile for a moment. How many times had Ashley smiled at Gabe before? And how many of those smiles had been real?

Mike took Gabe's money, counting it slowly, and then he slid the bills into his pocket. He reached over Bernetta's head and pulled a plain gray shoe box marked "Men's Brown Dress Shoe—Quality Leather" off one of the shelves. Inside was a stack of twenty-dollar bills. Mike plucked out ten and handed them to Gabe. "Here's your trial," he said. "Two hundred dollars counterfeit. If it works out for you, come back and you can place your order."

"And if it doesn't work out?" Bernetta asked.

Mike reached for the doorknob. "Then you never met me, and good luck in juvenile detention."

Bernetta looked at Gabe, and he raised his eyebrows at her.

As they filed out of the storeroom and left the store, ten of Mike's special twenties buried in Gabe's pocket, Val eyed them curiously. The bell clanged once again, and the door closed.

As soon as they were outside, Ashley pulled them behind the store, next to a Dumpster. "Hey, dimwad," she said to Gabe, "I want to get a good look at this money. Hand it over."

Gabe glanced at Bernetta, and she shrugged, so he handed Ashley the cash.

"It looks good, right?" Bernetta said, peering over Ashley's shoulder. "Pretty real."

"I'm *looking*," Ashley said. She held each one of the bills close to her eyes to inspect, and Gabe and Bernetta waited for her verdict, taking tense breaths. "Seems good," Ashley announced at last. "I can barely tell the difference myself, and I've had some experience with the stuff." Gabe snorted, but Ashley didn't seem to notice. She folded the wad in half and stuck it in her purse. "Let's try it out."

The plan was to hit up several different stores, find something cheap, preferably under a dollar, and pay for it with one of Mike's twenties. Then they'd collect the change and have made a very nice profit.

The choice of shops in the strip mall was limited, but within a half hour they'd managed to do pretty well for themselves. They bought a spool of thread in a crafts store, a soda in the doughnut shop, a "stone of healing" in a new age bookstore, and a yellow ballerina hair clip in a store that sold dance shoes and leotards. In each shop they handed the cashier one of the special bills, and other than the woman who sniffed at them when they began to examine tap shoes for toddlers, no one seemed to suspect anything out of the ordinary at all. Bernetta could feel herself breathing more calmly with every store they stepped into. It looked like everything was really going the way she and Gabe had planned.

Down to their last twenty, Bernetta, Gabe, and Ashley headed toward a kitchen supply store.

"Wait," Gabe said as they stepped toward the entrance. "I don't think we should go in that one."

"Why not?" Ashley said. "It's the only store left."

"Yeah, but—"

"Come on."

Ashley waltzed into the store, and Bernetta followed, with Gabe dragging behind them.

"Hello, kids," a woman in a blue apron greeted them. "Can I help you find anything today?"

"No, thanks," Ashley told her with a smile.

"Well, I'll be right over here if you—" She paused. "Why, hello, Gabe! I didn't even see you over there, behind all those pots and pans."

Gabe stepped out of hiding and cleared his throat. "Oh, hey, Denise. How's it going?"

"Pretty good. How's your uncle doing?" Gabe shrugged, hands in his pockets. "I'm a little worried about him lately. I hear he's thinking of getting back into show business."

"That's what he says."

"Well, we wish him the best. You know, Tim's in the back helping out today. I'm sure he'd love to say hi. Just a minute, I'll get him. Tim! Tim! Guess who's here!"

Ashley's face was slowly turning red. "What's *wrong* with you?" she hissed at Gabe. "You *know* that woman? How are we supposed to pull this off now?"

"She's a friend of my uncle's. What do you want me to do about it? I told you we shouldn't come in here."

"Who's Tim?" Bernetta asked.

"Just some kid I used to be friends with at school," Gabe answered. "He's Denise's son."

"Wait a minute," Ashley said. "Tim? Tim *Boucher*? Is that who it is?"

"Yeah," Gabe said. "So?"

"Who's Tim Boucher?" Bernetta asked.

"He's only the biggest dork at Harding Middle School," Ashley answered.

Bernetta fingered a chicken-shaped cookie cutter in a basket by the door. "He goes to Harding?" she asked.

Ashley snorted. "Yeah. He used to go to Kingsfield with me and Gabe, but then he moved. I heard he's captain of the chess club now. Can you believe that? Captain of the dorks is more like it. Come on. We should go before they—"

"Gabe!"

And there was Tim—well, Bernetta assumed it was Tim, by the way he was rushing out of the back room, heading full force for Gabe like he was a long-lost twin brother. Tim was tall and spindly, all arms and legs. His teeth were too big, and his eyes were too small. Ashley was right, Bernetta thought. He did sort of look like a dork. But a nice one.

"Gabe!" he called again. And when he reached him, the two boys did an awkward, highly complicated handshake that they'd probably made up when they were about nine. "Man! I haven't seen you in forever!"

"Yeah," Gabe replied, smiling. "How's it going?"

"Oh, you know," Tim said. He caught sight of Bernetta then and stuck out his hand, as though he wanted her to shake it. "Hi," he said. "I'm Tim."

"Um, Bernetta," she replied. It seemed weird to shake hands with someone her own age. Who did that?

He turned to Ashley next. "Tim," he told her, hand outstretched.

She scowled at him. "We've met," she said. "Mrs. Franklin's class?" Tim looked at her blankly. "I'm *Ashley*," she told him.

He shrugged and took his hand back. "Sorry," he answered. "I guess I don't remember you."

Ashley shot him a look of pure hatred. Bernetta definitely liked this Tim kid.

"Oh, man," Tim said, turning back to Gabe, "did you see that *Star Wars* marathon on TV last week? Do you remember when we memorized *Return of the Jedi* and acted it out for my parents? And I played Han Solo and you were Jabba the Hut?"

"Uh, I'm not sure I . . ." Gabe mumbled, glancing at Bernetta.

She just grinned. "Why would you memorize

Jedi?" she asked Tim. "Everyone knows that *Empire* is the best—"

"Jeez, are you *all* a bunch of morons?" Ashley exclaimed. "Sorry to break up the reunion, Jim, but we really should get going."

"Um, it's Tim," he said.

"Oh, really?" Ashley flashed her teeth. "Sorry. I didn't remember. Anyway, we just came in to get this." She grabbed the chicken cookie cutter from the basket and thrust it at Tim. "Could you ring us up, please? Thanks."

They paid for the cookie cutter, and Ashley dragged them out of the store after hurried good-byes to Tim and his mom. As they headed back to the shoe store, Ashley took the hair tie out of her hair and fixed her ponytail. "Well, *that* was horrible," she said to Gabe. "Aren't you glad that loser switched schools?"

"Yeah," Gabe answered, rolling his eyes in Bernetta's direction. "Real glad."

Was he was telling the truth? Bernetta slowed down for a moment, letting Ashley and Gabe walk a few steps ahead of her. Was it just her imagination, or were Ashley and Gabe actually stepping in sync with each other? Right foot, left foot, right foot, left foot . . .

Bernetta stopped walking.

When Gabe admitted he'd double-crossed her, had he told her the whole truth? Or was he still in cahoots with Ashley? Even now? Was he *triple*-crossing her? Was that even possible?

And how could you know who was on your side when the one person you'd decided to trust was someone you knew was completely untrustworthy?

Bernetta wondered for a moment what would have happened if she'd never met Gabe at all, if she'd never attempted to con her way back to Mount Olive. She would have ended up at Harding Middle School in September. Would she ever have run into Tim? Would they have been friends, discussing their favorite *Star Wars* movies? It was weird, thinking there was a whole alternate life out there, waiting for her. An entirely different Bernetta Wallflower she could have turned into.

"Come on, Carlotta!" Gabe called back to her. "We have to give Mike our deposit money!"

Bernetta shook her head and hustled toward the store. The alternate Bernetta was just a wisp of a thought in her brain. The real-life Bernetta had a job to do.

19

[flourish *n:* a bold or extravagant
gesture, performed in order to impress
an audience]

When they reached the shoe store, Ashley opened the door, and the bell clanged again.

"Why, hello there." Mike greeted them. "Did you decide to"—his eyes darted to Val, who was stacking shoe boxes in the corner—"buy the shoes?"

"We'll take them," Ashley said as Bernetta squeezed through the door behind her.

"Great," Mike said. "Hey, Val? Can you run and get me a coffee? Large, no sugar. Thanks."

She eyed him suspiciously but left the store. "So," Mike said when the door was completely closed, "how much you in for?"

Gabe spoke up. "Two hundred."

Bernetta nodded slowly. "That's two hundred for the both of us," she told Mike. "We're going in together."

Mike ran a finger over his mustache. "I'm going to all this trouble for two hundred *bucks*? Listen, kids." He lingered on that last word for a moment and then went on, "I usually deal with bigger numbers, if you catch my drift."

"Yeah, but, um," Bernetta said, "well, it would be more, but I don't have any money right now, 'cause it got, um, stolen. So Ga—*Alan* is lending me some, and then we're going to split the profit. And then we'll come back next week, and we'll be able to invest even *more*, and then . . ." She trailed off. She'd said it just right, exactly what she and Gabe had decided to tell Mike when he got fidgety with the deal. But suddenly Bernetta couldn't remember if it had been her idea to say those things or Gabe's. Had she been letting someone else put words in her mouth? What if none of this worked? Had this all been the stupidest idea she'd ever— "Oh." She realized Mike was staring at her, stroking his mustache, waiting for her to finish. "And um, then eventually I'll have enough to go back to school."

"That's a cute little story," Mike said. "But I'm afraid I—"

"I'm in for more," Ashley said. She flicked the tip of her ponytail over one shoulder.

"Yeah?" Mike said, leaning in across the counter. "How much more?"

Bernetta and Gabe leaned in too.

"Twenty," Ashley said.

Bernetta made an involuntary noise in her throat, a sound somewhere between a jet taking off and a raccoon drowning. "Twenty?" she asked.

"You heard me," Ashley replied, eyes fixed on Mike.

But Bernetta still couldn't believe it. "Twenty *thousand* dollars?"

Ashley rolled her eyes. "Yes."

"Oh." Bernetta turned to Gabe. His eyes were wide with shock too. "Oh, okay, yeah." She stuck her hands in her pockets, trying to act for all the world like twenty thousand dollars was a completely normal amount of money to hand over to a guy in a shoe store.

Mike drummed his fingers on the countertop. "You done gaping?" he asked Bernetta.

"Um, yeah."

"Good." He turned back to Ashley. "Now, I need your deposit today, in cash, and then you can come back tomorrow morning to pick up the bills."

Ashley squared her jaw. "Why can't you give it to us right now?"

"You think I have that kind of stash lying around?" Mike said with a laugh. "No. I work according to the laws of supply and demand."

"Good thing, too," Gabe put in, "'cause you're obviously not very good at selling shoes." Bernetta poked him in the ribs, and Mike shot him a stony glare, but Ashley ignored them all.

"Fine," she said. "Then we'll come back tomorrow to get the counterfeit cash. But no deposit."

Mike leaned down low, his hands gripping the counter and his shoulders bent at sharp angles. "Look, *girlie*," he told Ashley. "I don't make the bills, all right? That's Bruce's department. I just dole 'em out. So I don't think *Bruce* is gonna give me twenty thousand dollars' worth of merchandise if I don't have something to give him in exchange. You give me half today or it's off."

For a few moments it seemed like Ashley was thoroughly interested in her fingernails, examining each one in turn. Finally she took a deep breath and looked up again. "Fine," she told Mike. Then she unzipped her purse, and Bernetta watched as she pulled out a thick roll of bills, a rubber band wrapped tightly around it. She took off the rubber band and counted out the money. They were mostly twenties and some fifties and tens, but there were a lot of ones and fives and several hundreds sprinkled in there too. Ashley set every bill on the counter as she counted, and when she was done, Mike picked up the whole stack and counted again. It was exactly ten thousand dollars.

Gabe smacked one hundred dollars down on the counter, and Bernetta couldn't help noticing how piddly their pile looked next to Ashley's. "Our half," Gabe said.

Mike pulled a purple shoe box from underneath the counter and whisked all the money inside. "I'll see you kids tomorrow then," he said, dismissing them with a wave of his hand. "Store opens at nine."

They were just stepping out the door when Mike called to them again. "Hey, you, kid! What's your name, Alan?"

They turned.

"Yeah?" Gabe asked.

"What it says on your shirt, COFFEE, TEA, OR DEATH? That from a movie or something?"

Gabe raised an eyebrow. "Yeah. *Bait and Switch.*"

"Huh," Mike replied. "Thought so. That was a pretty good one. I like the part where the waiter kills the guy in the restaurant."

When they were safely outside, with the door closed behind them, Ashley climbed on her bike, but Bernetta stopped her before she could pedal away, hands firm on Ashley's handlebars.

"What's your problem?" Ashley asked her, yanking her bike backward.

"Where did you get twenty thousand dollars?"

Ashley glared at her. "None of your business. Now, if you two morons don't have any more field trips planned, I'm going home." She placed her feet on her bike pedals and lunged forward. Bernetta leaped out of the way just in time.

Gabe rolled his eyes as Ashley rounded the corner. "Tell me again why we were friends with that girl?" he said to Bernetta.

Bernetta just shook her head. It was funny, she thought. Her life had changed in at least a hundred ways in the past month, but she somehow was *still* hanging out with Ashley Johansson.

Something about that just didn't add up.

20

> 🖙 **simple vanish** *n:* an easy-to-perform
> sleight of hand used to vanish a coin

That night Bernetta couldn't sleep. It was too hot in her room. Much too hot. She kicked all the blankets and sheets off the bed, rolled her purple pajama bottoms up over her knees, and turned her pillow over so the cooler side would be against her cheek. But she was still wide-awake.

As the red numbers on her alarm clock switched from 12:36 to 12:37, Bernetta thought she heard a car pulling into the driveway. She padded across her room in her bare feet, pulled back her curtain, and checked outside.

Elsa's blue bug! She was back from camp.

Bernetta crept down the stairs as quietly as she

could, trying not to wake anyone up. She made it to the front door just as Elsa pushed it open.

"Elsa!" Bernetta cried, hugging her sister so hard that Elsa dropped her duffel bag. "I'm so glad you're home!"

Elsa laughed. "You didn't wait up for me, did you, Netta? It's so late."

Bernetta shook her head, nose still buried in her sister's shoulder. "I couldn't sleep." She let out an involuntary sniffle. "I missed you, Elsa."

"I missed you too." Elsa hugged her tight. "Netta, is everything okay?"

Bernetta took a deep breath and thought about how best to answer that question. The truth was, everything was *not* okay. She'd made a mess of things this summer, she knew she had. Counterfeit money? Running scams with a boy she hardly knew? Getting involved with Ashley again? Ashley *Johansson*?

"No," Bernetta said, shaking her head again. "No, it's not."

"Oh, Netta." Elsa pulled her back to get a good look at her. "What's wrong?"

"It's—it's just—" She noticed the duffel bag on the floor. The front door was still open. "It's nothing. You just got home. You probably want to go to sleep. Sorry. I don't even know what's wrong with me. I'm tired, I guess."

Elsa tucked a strand of her silky black hair behind her ear, still perfectly curled, even after midnight. "You're probably right; you just need some sleep." She leaned down and picked up her bag.

"How was camp?" Bernetta asked.

"It was good," Elsa replied. "Only . . ."

"Only what?"

"Only my feet are disgusting. Five weeks out in the forest, you know? I could really use a good toenail polish." She glanced at Bernetta. "Too bad you're so tired."

Ten minutes later they were stretched out on Elsa's floor. Elsa had changed into her pajamas, and she was painting her toes Georgia Peach. Bernetta rummaged through the dresser drawer, searching for the perfect color. She wasn't in the mood for Blueberry Bramble, it definitely wasn't a Tangerine Delicious evening, and she'd chucked the Rustic Red in the garbage.

"So?" Elsa asked. "What's going on?"

Bernetta took a deep breath and held it. She was practically bursting with all the things she wanted to tell her sister. Everything. All of it. All the lies and deceits and cons and Gabe and Ashley and every last detail. But she couldn't. For a second she wished she were still Same Old Netta, so she'd know exactly how to tell Elsa what she was feeling. So she wouldn't have any of these problems in the first place.

But she was a very different Bernetta Wallflower now. She let out all the air in her lungs and took a bottle of polish out of Elsa's drawer. Ruby Slipper. She examined it closely. Was the new Bernetta a Ruby Slipper kind of girl? She didn't know. Maybe. She placed the bottle on the floor and picked up another one. Perfect Plum Purple? Was that what she was feeling? Or was she more of a Midnight Frost?

"Netta?" Elsa asked, her voice soft. "You okay? What's wrong?"

Silver Bells? Easy Being Green? Twirly Girlie Grapefruit?

Bernetta grabbed all the bottles from the dresser and dumped them on the floor.

"Netta?"

Then, all at once, Bernetta gulped and sputtered, and the tears flooded out.

"I . . ." Bernetta said, her face in her hands. "I don't

know what color I want!" She couldn't help the tears.

Elsa rushed over to her and scooped her up in a hug. She held on tight for a long time. "Shh. Shh, Netta, it's okay. It's all right."

And Bernetta let her say those things, whisper them in her ear as if they were true. But really, were they?

It was several minutes before Elsa let her go. She rubbed Bernetta's arm softly. "Can you tell me what's wrong, Netta?"

Bernetta shook her head slowly, swallowing hard. How could she explain to Elsa that she'd spent the whole summer trying to be someone different, and now she didn't much like the person she'd turned into?

Elsa handed her a tissue, and Bernetta wiped her face. When she thought she had the sobbing under control, she attempted a smile, although it came out more as a sniffle than anything else. "Sorry," she said.

"That's okay," Elsa replied. "It's been a tough summer, huh?"

Bernetta rolled her wet tissue into a ball. "Yeah. I guess—I guess I missed you." She tossed the tissue toward Elsa's trash can, but she was short by two feet. "Sorry I'm such a mess. I should probably go to bed or something." But she stayed on the floor, staring blankly at the wall.

Elsa didn't say anything. She just got up slowly and crossed the room to her desk. When she came back, she was holding three sheets of paper, stapled together and creased into fourths. "I was going to give this to you when I left for college, but here." She handed the pages to Bernetta. "I think you need it now."

"What is this?"

"My valedictorian speech," Elsa said. "Go ahead. Read it. I'm going to paint your toenails. No peeking now."

Bernetta took the papers and read the first sentence while Elsa grabbed her left foot. *Good afternoon, friends and family, teachers, and fellow graduates.*

"What color are you painting them?" Bernetta asked from behind the speech.

"It's a surprise. Keep reading."

Thank you for sharing this occasion with us.

Bernetta skimmed ahead, doing her best not to look at Elsa or her own toes.

People say that these are the best days of our lives, but I know we all have many exciting adventures in front of us. Who knows what our futures hold?

Bernetta could feel the tears pinching at her eyes again. Why was her sister making her read this? So she'd know exactly how thrilled Elsa was about leaving for all her *exciting adventures*?

"Are you reading?" Elsa asked.

"Yes," Bernetta grumbled.

But as amazing as our futures will be, I think it's important to remember the things that shaped our past. I know I wouldn't be the person I am today—I wouldn't be up here right now—if it weren't for the people in my life who cared about me. The people who will stay with me no matter where life may take me.

Bernetta continued reading for a few more lines but then stopped. "Elsa," she said. "This is about me."

"Yeah, I know. I wrote it."

"Why would you write your valedictorian speech about *me*?"

Elsa swatted at Bernetta's leg. "No peeking, Netta! I told you! And I wrote the speech about you because you're my sister, and I'm going to miss you. And I wanted you to know how much you mean to me."

"How much *I* mean to *you*?"

"Yeah. Of course it would have been more dramatic and meaningful at graduation, if you'd heard me say it in front of everyone, but . . ."

Bernetta smiled. "This way works too," she said.

When she finished reading, she waited until Elsa painted the last of her toes, and then she asked, "Are you really going to miss me, Elsa?"

"Are you kidding? How many sisters do you think I have? You can look at your feet now, by the way."

Bernetta looked.

Elsa had painted each of her toes a different color—baby blue, yellow, cranberry, violet—ten different colors, one for each toe.

Elsa grinned at her. "I wanted to give you options," she told Bernetta.

Bernetta felt her tears melting away. "Thanks," she said. And she meant it.

Bernetta helped Elsa put the polish bottles back in the drawer, and when they were done, Elsa gave her another hug. But this one felt less squeezy big sistery and more comforting and understanding. "I don't know what's going on with you," Elsa told her, "but I'm sure you'll figure it out."

Bernetta looked down at her rainbow toes. "Maybe," she said.

"You will," Elsa replied. "You're the smartest person I know."

Bernetta thought about that as she snuggled into bed.

You're the smartest person I know.

Coming from Elsabelle Wallflower, school valedictorian, it was quite a compliment.

———

Somehow Bernetta overslept the next morning. When she woke up and saw the red numbers on her clock glaring at her, she jumped out of bed and raced to her dresser, yanking a T-shirt and shorts out of her drawer without even bothering to check if they matched. She slid her feet into a pair of flip-flops and raced out the door as she hollered good-bye to her parents. Then she pedaled into town as quickly as she could, her braid whipping out a rhythm against her back.

Ashley was already there, sitting on the stoop in front of the shoe store when Bernetta dumped her bike on the sidewalk. Gabe was nowhere in sight.

Ashley leaped to her feet. "Look!" she shouted. She did not sound happy. "Look at that!"

Bernetta looked to where Ashley was pointing. The sign in the window of the shoe store. THIS SPACE FOR SALE BY OWNER.

All the windows were covered in thick white paper.

Ashley's face was red and seemed to be swelling

like a balloon. Bernetta wiped her sweaty palms on her shorts and tried to think of something to say. "Um, I guess this means Mike—"

"He left!" Ashley hollered at her. "He's gone, and he's *stolen* our money!" She spat out the word "stolen" like it left a rotten taste in her mouth.

"Yeah," Bernetta said. She blinked. "Yeah, I guess he did."

Ashley threw her hands in the air. "Oh, what do you care anyway? You didn't even put in any money. I put in everything I had! *Everything*!" Ashley was screaming now, pacing back and forth.

"But you . . ." Bernetta said slowly. "That wasn't everything you had. You still have ten thousand dollars. The other half of your deposit."

Ashley came up close to Bernetta and stopped right in front of her, her face just inches away. "There wasn't any more money. I lied."

"Oh," Bernetta said. "I—I didn't know that."

Ashley began pacing again. "This is all your fault," she said.

"What?" Bernetta hollered. She could feel her face getting hot now. "How is this my fault?"

"I wouldn't be here if it weren't for you! I wouldn't

have lost all my money!"

"Well, *I* wouldn't be here if it weren't for *you!*" Bernetta screeched back.

There was more she could have said, much more, about friendship, and school, and trust, and . . . everything, really. All the mean, terrible, awful things that had been boiling inside her head for weeks now. But she didn't say it, not any of it.

Because at that moment she glanced down at her feet and caught sight of her toes—ten different colors. *I wanted to give you options*, Elsa had said.

And all of a sudden Bernetta realized that she *did* have options—dozens of them, maybe even hundreds. A whole rainbow of options. Maybe she couldn't control if her sister moved away. Maybe she couldn't control if someone stole from her or if the people she thought were her friends turned out to be con artists and backstabbers. But there were some things she *could* control. There were a million alternate Bernettas she could become, and she wasn't going to get roped into becoming one she didn't like.

Bernetta climbed back on her bike slowly and took a good long look at the abandoned shoe store, chewing on her lip. Then she turned to Ashley.

"Well?" Ashley cried, her hands on her hips. "Don't you even *care*? I lost ten thousand dollars! Do you know how much money that is? Aren't you going to say *anything*?"

Bernetta set her feet firmly on her bike pedals and thought about the one thing she should say to Ashley Johansson. Then, her mind made up, she said it.

"Good-bye, Ashley," she told her. And she pedaled away.

21

> ☞**switch** *v:* to exchange one object for another secretly

B ernetta took a deep breath as she pulled her bike in front of 173 Fields Street, parked on the sidewalk, walked across the grass, and knocked on Gabe's door. It opened almost immediately. But it wasn't Gabe who opened it.

"Why, hello there, Carlotta!"

"Hey, *Mike*," she said. Then she tilted her head to the side and grinned. Gabe's uncle Kevin looked a whole lot different without his mustache.

He ushered Bernetta inside. "How did it go with your friend?" he asked as they made their way into the living room.

"Who, Ashley?" Bernetta shrugged a shoulder.

"Well, she's not exactly my friend anymore. But I guess it went okay."

Uncle Kevin nodded. "Do you know she called and left a message on the store machine last night, saying that she'd be there early to pick up the money for all three of you? You believe that? The two of you put in nothing compared with her, and she still tried to cheat you out of it."

Bernetta just shook her head.

Gabe walked into the living room then. "Hey! Bernetta!" he cried. "I thought I heard you. Uncle Kevin, why didn't you tell me Bernetta was here? So how did it go? Did she buy it? Are we in the clear?"

"Don't worry," Bernetta said. "You probably won't have to fake your own death or anything."

"Oh, good," he said. And then he hugged her. He wrapped her right up. They stayed like that a moment, with Gabe's arms tight around her and Bernetta's out loosely to the side, not sure if she should hug him back or not, and then all of a sudden Gabe pulled away. He smiled at Bernetta but quickly glanced down at his sneakers, his cheeks turning red. "Uh, anyway . . ." He turned to Uncle Kevin. "So can we see it now?" he asked. *"Please?"*

"The money?" Uncle Kevin laughed. "Yeah, it's right there by the door."

Gabe located the purple shoe box and scooped it up off the rug. He motioned to the couch, and together the three of them sat down. They stared at the box for a moment in silence, until finally, slowly, Gabe removed the lid.

"Wow," Gabe whispered. "Ten thousand dollars."

"Ten thousand one hundred," Uncle Kevin corrected.

Gabe's eyes were wide. "Either way," he said, "it's a lot of money."

Bernetta peered into the box. It was a lot of money all right. Somehow it looked like even more money than when Ashley had taken it out of her purse. Bills upon bills, green and yellow and tan, a few with folded edges and others nice and crisp.

Gabe reached into the box and leafed through the bills. "Here," he said, handing a stack to Uncle Kevin. "This is for you. Eleven hundred bucks. The hundred dollars you lent me for the deposit, plus the money for the trial twenties, and then a little something for your acting gig. Bernetta and I decided you should have it."

Uncle Kevin took the money and held it in his hand for a moment, as though weighing it. "Well," he said at last, "normally I'd say thanks but no thanks, you two are kids and all that. But today I think I'm going to take it. I need it now that my store's busted and I'm trying to reboot my life back in Hollywood." He smiled at Bernetta. "You know," he told her, "if you wanted to, I think you'd make a pretty good actress. You've got a lot of talent, if you ask me. Although"—he pulled his wallet out of his back pocket and wedged the money inside—"it looks like you're already doing pretty well for yourself."

"I know, right?" Gabe said. "Man, I can't believe we made so much money. You were *good*, Bernetta. You're like the next Al Capone."

Al Capone? Bernetta thought. Didn't Al Capone kill people? She looked down at her rainbow toes and gave them a good wiggle.

Gabe finished counting through the bills. "Yep, nine thousand dollars. It's perfect." He set the lid on the box and held it out to Bernetta. "Exactly what you need to go back to Mount Olive."

"But . . ." Bernetta stared at the box in Gabe's outstretched hands. "I can't take all—I mean, it was your idea. It was your *uncle*."

Uncle Kevin laughed at that, and Gabe set the box in Bernetta's lap. "Let's just say we're even," he told her. He turned back to Uncle Kevin. "So, are you *really* moving back to Hollywood this time?"

"I really am," Uncle Kevin replied, setting his hands firmly on his knees. "I'm shipping out in just a few days. Good thing you kids caught me when you did. Actually, I should probably get going. I still have a lot of loose ends to tie up before the big move." He stood up. "Thanks for the acting gig, Gabe. I appreciate it."

"No problem."

"Bernetta, it was lovely meeting you."

"Yeah." Bernetta was still staring at the purple shoe box in her lap. It was surprisingly heavy.

When Uncle Kevin had gone, shutting the front door behind him, Gabe turned back to Bernetta on the couch and tucked both feet underneath him.

"So what did Ashley say when she saw the store was closed?" he asked her, grinning. "Did she go all psycho-Gollum? Like when he bites off Frodo's finger inside Mount Doom? Oh, man, and do you remember when we were looking at those twenties? And Ashley was like, 'I can hardly tell they're counterfeit myself.' And that whole time Uncle Kevin had given us *real* twenties! And then when we were in the kitchen store and—"

"Gabe?" Bernetta said.

"Yeah?"

She tilted the purple shoe box in her lap, listening to the sound of the bills resettling themselves. "You think there's any way we could figure out who all those kids were at Mount Olive, who Ashley stole the money from? Maybe we could try to give it back."

"Maybe," Gabe said, shaking his head. "But wouldn't it be really hard to track down all of the—" He stopped talking and squinted at her. "Wait, why would you give it back? You need the money for school."

Bernetta curled all her toes up under her feet and then relaxed them again. "I think—" Rainbow toes, no rainbow toes. "I don't think I'm going back."

"*What?*" Gabe said. His chin was scrunched up in confusion. "What do you mean you're not going back? I thought that's what all this was about. That's why we were working this whole summer. And now you don't even want it?"

Bernetta sighed. She didn't know quite how to explain it. Five weeks ago she'd thought she'd give anything to go back to Mount Olive. But now that she knew exactly what that *anything* was . . . well, it just didn't seem like the best option anymore.

Gabe shook his head. "So you're going to Harding instead then?"

"Yeah," she said. "I guess so. Yeah."

"Oh," Gabe replied. He was silent for a moment, staring off at his shelves full of movies. "Well, then does that mean—does that mean you're retiring too?"

"Retiring?" Bernetta asked.

"From the con artist business. Are you done for good?"

Bernetta curled her toes up again. "Yeah." Saying the word felt surprisingly good, like letting out a breath of air she'd been holding so long that her chest ached. "Yeah, I'm retiring. You're not mad at me, are you?"

"Why would I be mad at you?"

"'Cause, you know, you're going to have to find a new partner now. Bonnie and Clyde and everything."

Gabe just laughed. "A new partner?" He flopped back onto the couch, like he'd just let out a huge breath himself. "Nah," he said. "I think I'm going to retire too."

"Really? But I thought you loved being a con artist."

He shrugged one shoulder. "It's not really the same as in the movies, you know?"

Bernetta nodded and clutched the shoe box tight between her hands. "Well, I guess I should get going."

"Okay," Gabe replied. "You wanna come over tomorrow? Now that we're retired, you can get caught up on all those films you need to see. I think

I'm going to show you *The Godfather* first."

"Actually, Gabe, I"—she stood up, and he did too—"I don't know if I can. I'm sort of supposed to be grounded for the summer."

"Oh," he said. "Okay. Well, maybe when school starts again? You could come over on weekends or something?" He cleared his throat. "If you want to, I mean. You don't have to."

She laughed. Suddenly she realized that maybe Gabe didn't always know what to say to her either. "I think I'd like that," she told him.

"You know," Gabe said as they headed to the front door, "if you go to Harding, maybe you can hang out with Tim. You guys could be copresidents of the chess club. Then Ashley could make fun of both of you at once." He grinned. "It would save her a lot of time."

When they reached the door, Bernetta paused, her hand on the doorknob. Was he going to try to hug her again? Should she hug him?

"Well," he said, "'bye, I guess."

"'Bye," Bernetta replied. She opened the door and stepped outside.

She walked down the steps and across the grass, and she had just reached her bike when Gabe called out to her.

"Bernetta?"

She whirled around. Gabe was standing in his doorway, hands in his pockets.

"Yeah?"

"I was just thinking. Maybe I could try to get kicked out of Kingsfield. Do something really awful. Then I could hang out with you and Tim at Harding."

Bernetta placed the shoe box delicately inside the front basket of her bike and climbed up on the seat. Then she looked up at Gabe and smiled.

"Try not to live up to all my expectations," she told him.

He smiled right back. *"The Sting,"* he said with a nod. "I told you it was a good movie. You'll like *The Godfather* even better."

"See you, Gabe."

"See you."

She rode off down the street. And with each pump of her pedals, life for the new Bernetta Wallflower began to seem more and more exciting. No more cons, no more secrets, watching *The Godfather* on the weekends, even Harding Middle School didn't seem so bad anymore. Maybe she'd even join the chess club like Gabe had said.

Yes, Bernetta thought as she turned the corner. She'd probably be awfully good at chess.

22

> **☞ center tear** *n:* a trick in which a magician communicates a message written on a piece of paper that has been previously folded, ripped, and burned

After Bernetta had deposited her money in the bank, she wandered around town for a while, pedaling in lazy zigzags across the street. She went to the park and bought an ice-cream bar from the truck on the corner and sat on a bench in the playground while she ate, her rainbow toes stretched out far in front of her. All around her kids were playing, skidding down the slide headfirst or turning flips on the parallel bars or whispering to each other under the shade of a tree. A group of girls her age was playing soccer on a wide stretch of grass, and some teenagers were having a makeshift picnic of sodas and potato chips, stretched out on their stomachs reading magazines.

This was summer, Bernetta realized. And she'd missed it. She'd been too busy trying to get somewhere else.

Bernetta pulled the change from her ice-cream bar out of her pocket and plucked out one quarter, holding it in her left hand. She raised it to chest level, as though demonstrating the coin to a captive audience. And as the sun stretched its way across the sky and the warm afternoon drifted into breezy early evening, Bernetta practiced the French Drop.

========

Colin was bouncing a ball against the garage door when she pulled into the driveway.

"Hey, Bernie Bernie!" he called to her as she set her feet on the ground to stop herself. "I get to go to Zack's for a sleepover. He has a guinea pig. Also, Elsa says I can't own my own planet until I'm eighteen. Is that true?"

Bernetta parked her bike against the garage and scooped Colin up into a hug, lifting his feet right off the ground.

"What was that for, Bernie Bernie?"

She set him back down and shrugged. "Nothing," she said. "I like you, that's all. Plus I wanted to say thanks. For being such a good roper with Ashley."

"Oh," Colin said. "You're welcome. What's a roper?"

"The person who brings in the mark," Bernetta told him.

"What's a mark?"

She laughed. "I'll tell you when you're older."

"When I own my own planet?"

"Yes," she said, tousling his hair. Then she walked inside and upstairs to her room, feeling better than she had in a long time.

———

That night, when Bernetta's mother got back from dropping Colin off at his sleepover, Bernetta sat down for dinner with her parents and Elsa. Once everyone had ample amounts of food on their plates, Bernetta cleared her throat.

Her dad looked up.

"I want to show you guys something," she said.

She pulled a quarter from her pocket and, just as she'd practiced, held it up in her left hand and brought her right hand over, pretending to make the switch. She followed her right hand with her eyes the whole time, careful not to give anything away, and then opened her right hand to reveal that it was empty.

Her family began to applaud but stopped when Bernetta opened her left hand: empty as well. She could tell by the look on her dad's face that he hadn't been expecting that. No one else had either.

Slowly, Bernetta reached over her head, and from the depths of her massive braid of frizzy orange-yellow hair, she produced a quarter.

Her father dropped his napkin on the table and clapped his hands. "Bernie!" he cried. "That was amazing!"

"It really was," Elsa agreed.

"Truly excellent, Bernetta," her mother declared.

"Thanks," she said. Then she took a deep breath. A very deep breath. She set the quarter down on the table and stared at it for a moment. "Um . . ." She slid the quarter back and forth a fraction of an inch with her index finger. "Um . . ."

"Bernetta?" her mom said. "Is everything okay?"

She looked up. There was her mother, and her father, and Elsa. Waiting.

What would happen to the money, she wondered, the nine thousand dollars in stolen cash she'd deposited in the bank that afternoon? Maybe it could be donated to charity, to help kids with cancer or something, or to help train dogs find people buried under avalanches.

"Bernetta?"

She didn't know what they would do when she told them. When she explained all the way back to the beginning, about Ashley and the cheating ring. When she talked about Gabe, and the stealing, and all about the fake babysitting job and how she'd tricked Colin into helping her, and the long con they'd pulled, with Ashley as the perfect mark. There'd be yelling, that was for sure. Shouting too and crying—lots of crying. Lectures. Even more grounding. She'd probably have to see some kind of therapist or something, and they'd watch her like hawks, and maybe they wouldn't ever trust her again.

"Netta? What's going on?"

But when she told them, they'd *know*. No more secrets. No more lying. No more Bonnie, or Al Capone. Just Bernetta. Bernetta Wallflower. She had lots of choices, and she was determined to make the right one.

"Bernie?" her father said. "You all right?"

Bernetta nodded, and in one swift rush she let out the breath she'd been holding. "Yeah," she said. "I'm all right. But there's something I need to tell you guys."

It was time to lay her cards on the table.